THE LADIES' KILLING CIRCLE

A Crime & Mystery Collection

**Edited by Victoria Cameron
and Audrey Jessup**

Published by

GENERAL STORE
PUBLISHING HOUSE

1 Main Street, Burnstown, Ontario, Canada K0J 1G0
Telephone 1-800-465-6072 Fax (613) 432-7184

ISBN 1-896182-17-8
Printed and bound in Canada

Layout and Design by Leanne Enright
Cover Design by Tammy L. Anderson

General Store Publishing House gratefully acknowledges the assistance of the Ontario Arts Council and Canada Council.

Canadian Cataloguing in Publication Data

The ladies' killing circle: a crime and mystery collection

ISBN 1-896182-17-8

1. Detective and mystery stories, Canadian (English).
2. Canadian fiction (English)--20th century. 3. Crime-Fiction.
I. Cameron, Victoria II. Jessup, Audrey

PS8323.D4L34 1995 C813'.0108355 C95-900185-9
PR9197.35.D48L34 1995'

First Printing May 1995

ACKNOWLEDGMENTS

We thank the following for their assistance
in organizing and editing:

Joan Boswell

Victoria Cameron

Audrey Jessup

Mary Jane Maffini

Sue Pike

Madona Skaff

Linda Wiken

CONTENTS

Doomstones

Beneath these stones
Lies Mr. Jones,
Part of the garden walk.
No more the phone's
For Mr. Jones
From shapely Mrs. York.
Those wild hormones
Of Mr. Jones
Could have used a cork,
'Cause Mrs. Jones,
She broke his bones—
She'd heard the neighbours talk.
Now Mr. Jones
Wears nice flagstones—
Part of the garden walk.

Joy Hewitt Mann

THIS LITTLE KILLER WENT TO MARKET

by Audrey Jessup

Maria walked slowly back along the row of stalls. Crowds thronged the sidewalk, and she sidestepped as often as she moved forward. Tony had insisted everything must be perfect for his guests tomorrow though, so she figured she'd better check every stall before buying.

The corn on the end stall near York Street looked the best—fat, juicy yellow kernels. If she took two dozen, that would allow two per person with four over which she could use in an antipasto. She wove her way back towards the centre of the row. There was a stall opposite Lapointe's Fish Market which had wonderful green and red peppers, big and shiny. She'd need a lot for the pizzas she was making for lunch, and she could roast the rest on the barbecue before Tony cooked the steak and corn for dinner. She liked to have roasted peppers in the freezer and this was about as cheap as they'd get this year.

She needed romaine lettuce for the Caesar salad, and a big basket of beefsteak tomatoes for the appetizer of sliced mozzarella with tomato sprinkled with basil.

Maria made her way along to the stall that always kept fresh herbs in galvanized metal buckets on the sidewalk. She picked up a bunch of basil and sniffed, relishing the fragrance. She'd take two bunches. That should make enough pesto sauce for the winter. They didn't use as much as most Italian families because Tony couldn't eat it. He even hated the smell. Imagine an Italian allergic to basil. But it was certainly the only one of life's pleasures he missed out on.

The tap on her shoulder made her jump.

"Maria, come sta? We haven't seen you for a long time. You look as if you're shopping for an army." Lucia looked at Maria's shopping cart with its big bunches of basil waving merrily on top.

Maria laughed and gave her friend a hug. She and Lucia had gone to school together when they grew up near Preston Street. "This is a surprise, Lucia. I didn't think you ever came into the Ottawa market now you've moved to Orleans."

"I don't very often, but Claudio's mother wanted to visit a friend in the Elisabeth Bruyère Hospital, so I thought I'd have a look at the market for old times' sake." She looked around. "They look like the same people behind the counters."

Maria laughed again. "At least you can always be sure there'll be lots of Cléroux from Navan running stalls. Do you have time for a coffee?"

Lucia looked at her watch and made a face. "Mi dispiace, no. I told Mamma I'd be waiting outside the front door of the hospital in five minutes. And she's always on time. Besides, I don't like to leave Claudio with the kids for lunch. He gives them whatever they ask for," she said with a smile. "We have three now, you know." Lucia paused and looked at Maria's basket. "Does this load of food mean you've had quintuplets and I missed the announcement?"

"No," Maria smiled. "We're having some of Tony's business associates and their wives up to the cottage for the day tomorrow."

"Tony still wants to have an empire before he has kids, eh?" Lucia looked at her friend seriously. "You're going to be hitting thirty soon, Maria. If I were you, I'd anchor him down with a couple of bambinos before he flies too high and thinks he needs a trophy wife." She reached out and squeezed Maria's arm. "Oh, mama mia, look at the time. Gotta fly. Remember me to Tony the Hunk." Lucia leaned forward and kissed Maria on the cheek. "And listen to what I said. Don't give him the chance to run around." She laughed and waved as she went off to collect her mother-in-law.

"As a matter of fact," Maria said silently to her friend's retreating back, "I had thought of it." She pictured Lucia arriving home, her three children jumping up and down around her and Claudio giving her a hug, and her mouth tightened.

After one more stop for bread from Le Petit Gourmet, she trundled her shopping cart over to the car. Despite her protests, Tony had insisted she take his big station-wagon to the market. "Easier for loading," he'd said, overriding her objection that it was harder to park. He knew she didn't like driving such a big monster. Tony had gone up to the cottage yesterday evening in her Toyota. He wanted to start getting everything shipshape for their guests. At least, that's what he said. She couldn't check what time he arrived because there was no telephone in the cottage, and he didn't have his cellular phone with him. She put the car in gear and made another driver happy as she pulled out of the parking space.

Traffic was always thick around the market area on Saturdays in the summer, and it took her almost ten minutes to reach Sussex Drive and cross the Alexandra Bridge to Hull. Once she got onto Highway 5, though, it was clear sailing almost as far as Wakefield, and in Tony's powerful car she made good time. After that, the road was two lanes and winding, and she wasn't as comfortable as she would have been in her own smaller Toyota, but she knew the road well. They'd bought the cottage on 31-Mile Lake two years after they got married, and in the six years since then they had made a lot of improvements. She'd hate to lose it. She put her hand up to her shirt pocket. The paper was still there. A receipt in the amount of $156.00 for satin sleepwear from Victoria's Secret in Washington. She'd seen the ads for their garments, always gorgeous and alluring. When she'd found the receipt last month, she'd been thrilled. She thought Tony was going to surprise her with lovely, sexy lingerie for their eighth wedding anniversary. He'd surprised her all right. With a great flourish, he'd presented her with an electric bread-making machine. It could mix the bread and even bake it while she was at the office. Quella gioia!

It wasn't fair, she thought. She had always tried hard to keep herself looking good. Looks were very important to Tony. She hadn't put on more than three pounds since they got married, and that was a real effort when she was always cooking big Italian meals for Tony and his friends. She tried to dress well, especially as Tony's construction business started to grow and she had to accompany him to dinners and business conventions. The only thing she hadn't been able to do was give him a child.

Lucia had been right. At first Tony didn't want a family until he'd established himself, and he was quite happy for her to continue working as an executive assistant. The money was good, and he thought it had prestige. But two years ago, he'd wanted her to quit and stay home to raise children, which she was quite willing to do, as soon as she became pregnant. But she hadn't become pregnant, and the subject hadn't been mentioned for more than five months—ever since Tony went to Washington for the first time with that group of government and industry people. And now he'd given her a bread-maker. That was where he saw her in his life. In the kitchen.

It would be like that this weekend. The four couples Tony had invited were part of a new crowd he was cultivating. The men were always talking about their latest deal, and the women about the latest thing they'd bought for themselves, their house, or their kids. Two of them were what Lucia would call "trophy wives," married within the last year after their husbands had gone through acrimonious and expensive divorce proceedings. Divorce, of course, was not an option for Tony or her with their very strict Catholic families.

A horn blared and Maria yanked the wheel over, horrified to find she'd been drifting towards the centre line. This was a dangerous highway. It didn't do to get too preoccupied. On her right the Gatineau River sparkled in the sun. It looked lovely, but a plunge down the bank into its cold waters would not be so inviting. She shivered and concentrated on her driving.

She turned off the highway for the road to the cottage and stopped at the general store in the village.

"Bonjour, Maria." The proprietor's wife smiled her welcome. "Tony was just in for gas for the barbecue. And beer, of course. Having a big party tomorrow, eh?"

"Yes, so I need lots of ice cream. You know how Italians are for ice cream, Louise," Maria laughed. "And they're saying the temperature might hit thirty."

As she bent over the freezer making her selection, Louise chattered to her back. "I was happy to see it was Tony driving the Toyota, not you. Jacques saw the car come in last night, well, this morning, really, about 2 a.m., and I know you don't like driving at night on the highway."

Maria felt her heart go as cold as her hands in the freezer, but she managed a smile as she straightened and put her purchases on the counter. Fortunately, Louise was too busy ringing up the sale to pay attention to Maria's expression.

"Un chocolat, un vanille, et deux spumoni pour Tony." Louise laughed. "He must eat a gallon of it every weekend in the summer."

"Winter, too," Maria said, packing the ice cream into the insulated bag she'd brought in with her. "And he still keeps his figure. There's no justice." She smiled at Louise and hoisted the bag in her arms. "Arrivederci," she called as she went out.

She managed to drive away from the store, but once she reached the top of their private road, she had to stop. Her hands were trembling and her jaw was clenched so tight it hurt. She knew where Tony had been until two in the morning. He'd been at her place. Maria knew who she was. And even what she looked like. After the first trip to Washington, Tony had been excited talking about the other people in the group, and one name kept coming up: Nadia Leman, a government economist.

"She's really bright," he said. "And funny, too. All the men liked her."

"Just the men?"

"No, no, I meant all the people," he'd blustered. "You're always looking for things to pick on."

After that he hadn't mentioned her name, although Maria knew Nadia had been on two other trips he'd taken. And he'd started going to more "meetings" in Ottawa. In the evening.

She'd looked up Nadia's address in the telephone book and one day after work she'd driven to her apartment. She was going to pretend she had the wrong floor or something, so she could get a look at her. But she hadn't needed to do that. Just as she arrived, Tony's car pulled up and a tall, long-haired blonde got out carrying an elegant burgundy leather briefcase. She'd bent down for a final word through the driver's window and as she turned away, Tony had caught her hand and kissed it.

This gesture sent Maria into a shaking, despairing rage which gradually turned into the deep cold anger she had felt congealed in the pit of her stomach every day since. She'd hoped it would be just a flash-in-the-pan affair, but it had been almost six months now, and he was still sneaking off to be with her. Even this weekend, when he wanted to have everything perfect for his important guests, he could spend half the night playing around with her. Maria felt the heavy clot of her rage churning and turning from ice into a burning fire like molten lava. She held her stomach and bent over the steering wheel, fighting the pain. She couldn't, she wouldn't, take it any more. It was several minutes before she could compose herself to continue down the lane to the cottage. Tony was putting out the garden chairs as she drew in. He'd turned the Toyota and left it near the entrance to their property, facing out, so she was able to drive the big car in close to the cottage, which was easier for unloading. As she climbed out, Tony came over and gave her a perfunctory kiss. He looked tired. No wonder.

"I'll bring the stuff in," he said.

They unloaded the car in silence and Maria put away the groceries. She placed the ice cream in the freezer, and stood staring at the home-made pizza bases she had stacked there: two marked "P" for pesto and two marked "T" for tomato. Her hand hovered for a moment, then she reached in and picked up a package marked "P", keeping her thumb over the tell-tale letter until she could unwrap it and crunch the paper up in the garbage. She took a jar of homemade tomato sauce from the refrigerator and spooned it over the green pesto sauce, cloaking the colour completely. While the oven heated, she cut up peppers, mushrooms, onions, and pepperoni. This was going to be a pizza he couldn't resist. She set a bunch of basil in a jar of water and placed it on the counter near the table. If Tony's sensitive nose picked up an aroma of basil as the pesto sauce cooked, he'd think it came from the fresh herb.

"I forgot to get the milk and cream," Tony said when she called him in for lunch. "Would you go for it afterwards, while I finish trimming the hedge?" Maria nodded. "I turned the car around because I was going to go back," he said. "But then I thought I might as well wait in case there was anything else you needed. The gas is still in the back seat, but it'll be okay until later."

Maria nodded again. "I think I'll have a glass of wine with my lunch," she said. "There's a beer out for you."

"Bene, bene." Tony sat down and pulled the glass towards him. "Boy, the pizza looks great. I'm starving." He picked up a slice and took a couple of bites from the tip. "Mmm. Good," he said, washing it down with a gulp of beer.

Maria carefully cut off a piece of her pizza and chewed it as she watched him.

"What time did you get here last night?" she asked, keeping her tone casual.

Tony took another large bite of pizza and mumbled, "Eight . . . nine."

Maria ate another mouthful of pizza, as Tony drank some more beer and finished his first slice. He lifted his second piece up, but just as he got the tip into his mouth he fell sideways off the chair. He lay on the floor, his eyes rolling in desperation, the pizza hanging out of his mouth like a green and red mottled tongue.

His hand reached up and flung the pizza away. "Maria," he croaked. "Basilico." He clutched his throat. "Mi sento morire."

Maria jumped to her feet and stood looking down at him. "Die then," she said through clenched teeth. "Muori, dannato. I'll see Nadia's invited to the funeral. She'll look wonderful in black."

Tony's brow beaded with sweat. He clutched at the chair and tried to pull himself up, but the feet slipped on the smooth floor and he fell back. "Phone . . . " He clutched his throat.

"I can't phone," Maria said. "I took the cellular out of your briefcase because I didn't want you sitting up here phoning her all last night." She laughed bitterly. "But you didn't need to phone her, did you? You only had to look over to the other side of the bed."

Tony's eyes rolled frantically. "C . . c . . car," he rasped. "Don't . . . take . . . "

"No, I won't take long," Maria said. "I'll use the phone at the store, and I'll get Jacques to come down and help me load you into his van to take you to the hospital. It'll be too late by then, of course. But it's what people expect. And maybe I'll even be able to cry, remembering the early years, when I was still good enough for you."

Tony lifted a hand towards her, his eyes beseeching, then his chest heaved, his breath rattled in his swollen throat, and his hand fell to the floor as his head rolled back.

Maria brought a cushion from the easy chair and put it under his head. She stared down at him, and the anger slowly faded from her face to be replaced by inexpressible sadness.

She snatched up her keys from the counter and hurried out to the Toyota. The car was hot. Tony had left the windows up. She rolled down the window on the driver's side.

When she turned the ignition key, the force of the explosion blew out the others.

ONE COLD COOKIE

by Joan Boswell

"Richard, that was perfect." I trailed my fingers through his hair. "We should be together all the time."

Richard mumbled something unintelligible into the pillow.

"Why don't you move in with me?" I persisted.

Richard rolled over. "You know I can't. Cally would be devastated, and the kids would never forgive me." He reached for my hands. "I know it's hard for you. It's really unfair. But, after all these years, I owe it to her to stay married as long as that's what she wants."

I didn't care what the stay-at-home cow wanted. This wasn't the first time Richard had said he couldn't leave her, but I had wanted to give him one last chance before making my decision. I prided myself on being fair.

Even in my ascent through the ranks of career civil servants, I'd been fair. I learned how to get what I wanted, and I left a few bodies behind on my way up to Assistant Deputy Minister, but I'd been fair. And I didn't have a single regret. It's a dog-eat-dog world.

Really, Richard left me no alternative. At thirty-eight I'd reached the point where the single life had lost its charm, the number of eligible men decreased daily, and Richard met my standards for a husband. Good-looking and amusing, the perfect escort, he charmed everyone.

Standards? Charm? Lies. Rationalizations. I might as well admit it. I was besotted; totally, absolutely crazy about him and, no matter what the cost, he was going to be mine, all mine.

Richard came into my life when the government awarded his company an initial contract to do a project for my department. After we'd worked together for weeks and spent a couple of noon hours in anonymous hotels, Richard claimed to have fallen in love with me. In my opinion, the excitement of an illicit affair, my gold credit card, and the fact that I taught him a thing or two in bed turned him on. Love had nothing to do with it.

To keep him dependent, I made sure he knew that without me his firm wouldn't be given preference when their contract came up for renewal. I had him, but I wanted more.

If we were going to be married, Cally had to go. All I had to do was figure out the perfect way to kill her.

Early in January, Richard unwittingly provided the answer. We'd spent an entertaining lunch hour bedded down in the Chateau Laurier. Curled together, I stroked his back while I surreptitiously checked my watch and discovered I had twenty minutes to get to an important meeting. I sat up and reached for my clothes; Richard pulled me back.

"I've got great news. Cally's going on the Canadian ski marathon in February." He squeezed my hands and smiled. "February fifteenth and sixteenth to be exact. I don't know if you've heard about it, but it's a two-day, hundred-mile, cross-country trek. It runs from Lachute to Gatineau." His smile turned into a grin. "Cally's hooked up with some women friends and, typical Cally, she's determined she's going to ski three sections, more or less thirty miles, each day. That's one heck of a lot of skiing. She's going to have to work like hell to get into shape. You know what that means? We're going to spend a lot of Saturdays and Sundays together while she practises."

"Wonderful." I murmured, bending to kiss our entwined hands. We'd never talked about skiing. Richard didn't know that three years before I'd covered the entire hundred miles of that same marathon and won a coureur de bois medal. I gave up competitive skiing once I'd proved my superiority, but I knew I still had the stamina to outski almost anyone.

At home that night, I found the marathon's phone number in the Yellow Pages. Even though I'd never given my valuable time, I knew they relied on volunteers to keep the event going. Distasteful though it was, the time had come. I phoned and said I wasn't going to ski, but I'd be glad to work in the office organizing the kits that went out to each entrant.

A few days later Richard phoned, "Would you be interested in spending marathon weekend in Montreal? Maybe staying at Place Bonaventure?" He laughed, "I hear their room service menu is quite spectacular."

"Sounds fabulous." I agreed.

"You may be sick of me by the end of the weekend," he said.

"Never," I said. Little did he know of my intention of making him mine forever.

However, to possess him for life, I had to forfeit the weekend. At the last minute, I'd invent a crisis to justify not showing up on Friday. Meanwhile, I had other things to do. I intended to cover my ass, to make sure that, whether it succeeded or failed, nothing linked me to Cally's death.

February arrived. On Tuesday, the eleventh, I told several people that my mother had messed up my weekend by insisting I drive her to Belleville on Friday to be with my aunt who'd just had an operation. I grumbled about the fact that she wouldn't drive in the winter and didn't want to take the train. Although some commiserated with me, I noted those whose faces reflected pleasure that my plans had unravelled. On Monday I'd make their lives unpleasant.

When I told Richard about my mother, I said I'd come to Montreal late on Saturday and planned to make up for the lost night.

His initial disappointment gave way to anticipation. "I'll be ready. We can take all the time in the world because Cally says she won't finish until at least five on Sunday."

Little did she know.

After work on Friday I unpacked the kit I'd stolen from the marathon office and found I'd be wearing bib number 3890. As I passed through the check-points, the volunteers would note the number, but, if anyone ever tried to match numbers and names, it wouldn't correspond to a name in the files.

I couldn't risk staying in a Lachute hotel in case someone recognized me. Instead, I rose at three on Saturday morning in order to reach the starting line by eight. Fortunately my car, a grey, late-model Ford, was not an attention getter. I ate breakfast and packed juice into my knapsack along with extra clothing, a spare ski tip, mylar sheet, and everything else skiers carry to keep themselves alive in the wilderness.

At seven-thirty, after a three-hour drive, I arrived in the parking lot of the sports field in Lachute where the race started. I unloaded my skis and poles, and strapped on my backpack. A bitter wind swirled the snow into whirlwinds which sliced and cut at exposed flesh. It was no day to stand around. I wore nondescript ski clothes; a balaclava which covered my face, ear muffs, and wrap-around, tinted ski goggles. My own mother wouldn't have picked me out of a police line-up. I tied on the purloined bib and became number 3890.

Marathon officials recorded the bib numbers of those who began and those who completed a ten-mile section. Because the hundred-mile route passed through snowy uninhabited Quebec wilderness, it was important to know who was on the trail. Checkers matched the numbers on the bibs to the lists and, if they found a discrepancy, alerted the sweeps, the people on snowmobiles who patrolled the route.

Moving into position with the five or six hundred skiers massing behind the tape at the starting line, I edged through the throng and scanned the team skiers, those wearing bib numbers beginning with 5000, until I spotted Cally Ross, who I knew from my research was wearing bib 5516. Dressed in a navy anorak, knickers and hat, with pink ear muffs and a pink and purple fanny pack, she waited with her team. When the gun sounded, I slowed my faster pace and kept behind her. Double-tracked for almost its entire one hundred miles, the trail allowed speedy skiers to forge ahead. Many, when they could, chose to ski in the better track on the left.

At the end of the first ten-mile section, the very young, the old, the cold, and the exhausted called it quits and loaded onto chartered school buses waiting to shuttle them back to their cars and motels. Those planning to continue refuelled at the provisioning tables manned by volunteers and set off again. Cally began the next section at a steady pace.

My quarry, with me lurking well back, passed through the next check-point at one-fifteen. After they completed this section, many skiers headed for the buses. Five hours of skiing into blowing snow at subzero temperatures had taken its toll. Volunteers from the 31st Scout Troop provided vegetable soup, hot honey drink, cold water, chocolate-covered peanuts, and oatmeal cookies for the hardy souls who intended to continue. I swallowed a cup of soup, three glasses of honey drink, and tossed back several handfuls of chocolate peanuts.

At one-thirty, with half an hour to spare before the check-point closed and marathon officials allowed no one else to start the next section, Cally and I both passed the checkers and set out for the day's most difficult skiing. Facing into the wind, we climbed along beside a golf course and set out through steep, heavily wooded country heading for the Kilmar Road and the climb to the infamous bobsled run. The cold, the sleet, and the passage of hundreds of skis since the coureurs de bois began at dawn had iced the track and the down hills challenged even the most experienced. Depressions along the track marked the sites where the less skilful had fallen.

When Cally slackened her pace three miles into the section, it allowed those coming along behind us to pass. At three-fifteen we reached the

Kilmar road where yellow school buses, motors running, sat enveloped in clouds of exhaust. I watched Cally stop beside the race official waiting on the road.

The critical moment had arrived. Would she quit or go on? While I waited to see what she'd do, I bent to retie my boot laces. Finally, after an animated conversation punctuated by arm waving and pointing up the hill, she set off up the mountain at a steady pace.

When I reached the man, he peered at me. "How're you feeling?" He checked his watch. "You know that in ten minutes we close it down." He looked back the way I'd come. "I see a couple more out there, but after them that's it. Now, you're sure you're okay? The worst is still to come."

When I repeated that I felt terrific, he waved me on my way.

An hour later, at four-fifteen, the wind had picked up and the light had waned. Four skiers had passed me. From a vantage point on the mountain, I looked back and saw no one else coming along. Ahead, the trail hugged the side of a cliff and descended steeply before it plunged into a series of downhill runs. I watched Cally, using the left track, cautiously pick her way down the icy slopes. A turbulent river, black and noisy, flowed in the valley many hundred feet below her.

The time had come.

I zoomed into high gear and got behind her as she entered an open stretch with nothing but insubstantial alders between her and the river. I gave a mighty thrust with my poles, dropped them to free my hands, and shot along the track on her right. Counting on my velocity, I hurtled along and, as I came level with her, turned and pushed her with all my strength.

She teetered and only had time to say, "What the hell . . ." before she lost control and plunged over the edge, tumbling and cartwheeling towards the rocks and rushing water. I saw this as I fought to control my skis and snow plough to slow my momentum. Knowing I wouldn't get far without poles, I intended to ski back to retrieve them.

But something went wrong. The pitch and depth of the tracks made snow ploughing impossible, and I kept accelerating. I knew I should fall, but while I hesitated the track emerged at a clearing. Totally out of control, I flew from the track and shot over a heavily crusted sloping field. In slow motion a massive oak tree filled my vision.

When I regained consciousness, it was dark and I lay half-buried in a snow bank. From the angle of my skis and the pain in my ankle, I suspected

I'd broken a bone. I listened to the faint sound of rushing water which I could hear over the keening wind. I heard nothing else: no cry from my victim; no sounds of rescue; just wind and water.

Cold penetrated my snow-dampened clothes. I told myself that the sweeps would come along any minute. When they saw where her tracks left the trail, they'd locate Cally or her body. The two sets of poles would tell them two skiers had collided and they'd search for me. However, rocketing across the smooth crust I wouldn't have left any tracks. No one would hear me shouting in this wind. Unless I found some way to attract attention, no one would find me.

I wriggled around, cautiously undid the bindings and lifted my feet free. Moving my ankle hurt unbearably, but I clenched my teeth and kept working. I hauled my knapsack from my back, rummaged for an extra red sock to pull over the ski tip and, after a struggle, managed to stand the ski upright in the snow. The sweeps should see it when they shone their powerful flashlights around.

While I waited, I worked out my story. I'd say I'd lost control as I passed Cally and knocked her off the track. In an attempt to save her, I'd dropped my poles. If she lived, she'd say I pushed her.

I'd agree that I'd lost my balance and it sure must have seemed like a push to her.

My bib number came next. I'd claim that the marathon office had sent it by mistake and at the last moment I'd decided to go in the race. With all the volunteers who worked in the office, who could challenge me?

Why would an expert like me ski so slowly? I hadn't done any practice skiing, and my wax had given me trouble.

Had I forgotten anything? Later, I'd explain to Richard and the people at work that after I'd delivered my mother I'd had an overwhelming urge to ski.

My self-confidence returned as I worked out convincing explanations. This wasn't the first time I'd been in a tight spot and used my considerable intelligence to extricate myself. But where were the sweeps? Why didn't I hear them?

With a twinge of uneasiness I finally thought to check the fluorescent dial on my watch. Horror replaced all other emotion when I saw the time—6:45. The sweeps had come and gone and, because they didn't know I existed, wouldn't venture out again. They must have arrived while I lay unconscious.

Unless I did something, I'd freeze to death. Working with frantic haste, I yanked the reflective mylar sheet out of my bag, shoved it under me, and wrapped it around my legs. Improvising, I employed the spare ski tip as a minishovel and built a snow break. I edged myself around with my back to the icy blasts, pulled on all my extra clothes and stuck a sucrose pill in my mouth. I pushed my knapsack behind me and curled myself into a small ball. Huskies lived outside in northern winters doing this; why wouldn't it work for me?

How long would I be out here? No one involved with the marathon would come searching. When the checkers noted that number 3890 hadn't come through the last check-point, they'd get out their list of entrants and find no such number. They'd conclude that the person writing the numbers down had made a mistake, had recorded someone's number incorrectly. No hope there.

I tried to stop my chattering teeth, to ignore the numbing pain in my feet. No one knew I was skiing. Although the police might notice my abandoned car in the parking lot, they'd assume that it hadn't started and the driver had hitched a ride home. By Monday, when my mother or Richard or my staff began looking for me I would have spent a day-and-a-half in this snow bank. I'd gambled on eliminating Cally and having Richard forever. Cally was gone, but forever was getting shorter with each body-chilling minute. An unfamiliar feeling of resignation crept over me and I permitted myself a small wry smile. I'd told myself I'd get Richard or die in the attempt: it looked like I was going to do just that.

Reading Gaol

Mysteries are more than books
With crime in all its stages.

They keep the murderers safe for us,
Imprisoned in their pages.

Joy Hewitt Mann

DARK DAY IN DISTRIBUTION

by Mary Jane Maffini

I gotta tell you, Monday's the worst day I had in thirteen years of being a Grim Reaper. Starts bad, right off. My first number's a seventy-five-year-old inventor and she ain't ready to be snatched. Most numbers take one look at the robe, the cowl, and the scythe and scare themselves to death. Not this lady. She's too busy. She ain't ready. And she ain't scared neither. She's right in the middle of a big experiment so she tries to bargain. Suggests some names I could substitute. I have one hell of time snatching her and I'm thinking I might even need to use the scythe.

By the time I get to the Donut Dip for break, I'm still rattled. So then Benny drops this bomb.

Right in the middle of a chocolate-glazed donut, he comes right out with it. Something's wrong in Distribution, he goes.

I stop in mid-bite. What's he talking about? Benny's all excited, even for Benny. His eyes are wilder than usual and his nose is glowing. He's got chocolate icing dribbling down his robe and he don't even notice because he's too worked up.

You gotta believe me, he goes, the numbers are not ending up where they're supposed to. What do you mean, I go, trying to enjoy my donut, that's crazy.

I know about Distribution. I started next door in Administration, thirty-three years ago and got promoted to Reaper only after typing a couple million work orders on the old Underwood. Administration got a lot of dealings with Distribution. Mistakes just don't happen there.

It's true, he goes, a guy from Delivery seen Henry Hubbard Upstairs.

I almost choke. Henry Hubbard. Upstairs? It ain't possible. Henry Hubbard is a creep. Everyone knows Henry Hubbard made millions as a slumlord. He took money out of poor boxes, rigged his income tax, cheated his own family. Henry never done a good thing in his life. And he's dead now, I know because I snatched him myself and enjoyed every second of it. I dropped his tar-covered soul at Distribution and scrubbed the sludge off my hands afterwards. Henry was headed straight Downstairs. Pronto. Must be someone else, I tell Benny. Benny's hands are shaking, his coffee spilling on the orange formica. What if it ain't, he goes.

What's your problem, I go. But I'm staring at him. I know what his problem is. Being a Reaper is rough, the kids at the Children's, the teenagers in car wrecks, the young mothers in delivery rooms, even that old inventor who wasn't ready. You carry on with the job because you know everyone ends up where they're supposed to. Good guys Upstairs. Creeps Downstairs. Some middle-of-the-road people get put through Recycling.

Not Henry. Henry was definite Downstairs material.

Guy seen him, Benny whispers. Seen him strolling around Upstairs like he owned the place. Can't be, I tell him. Benny's white as coffee creamer. But what if it is, he goes.

It's ten-fifteen by now and time for the next snatch. I'm hoping it's an easy one.

Lunchtime, we agree, we'll check out Distribution.

Lunchtime comes and we're outside Distribution like we got business there. What brings you guys here, the Foreman wants to know.

No way I'm gonna tell him about Benny's crazy idea. Benny's on pretty thin ice as a Reaper anyways.

I lost my scythe, I go. We're checking around. Foreman looks at Benny who still got smears of chocolate on his robe so you can believe he'd lose his scythe. Foreman turns back to me and shakes his head. Hey, man, you slippin' or what? Go on in and look, he goes, climbing into his New Yorker.

We duck into the office and check the book. Sure enough. In black and white. Henry Hubbard. Destination: Downstairs.

Yeah, well, Benny goes, how come the guy seen him Upstairs? It ain't always easy dealing with Benny.

Delivery guy who seen Henry Hubbard is just a kid, having a smoke outside because Headquarters is a smoke-free workplace. Sure, I'm sure, he goes. You think I don't know Henry Hubbard? He owned the rathole I grew up in. Winter sometimes the heat wouldn't even be turned on. My mother used to sit and cry with her coat on, tears freezin' on her cheeks. Guy like that shouldn't be Upstairs.

You know, I go, I think I got it figured out. Same day I snatched Henry I had another guy looked a lot like him. Same kind of shiny bald head, same ear hair, same belly. Only this guy Elvin McKinley was a volunteer over the homeless shelter and the food bank. The day I snatched him he was spending time with some guy dying of AIDS. More worried about that guy than himself. Musta been him you seen Upstairs.

Kid shakes his head. It's Henry Hubbard all right, he goes. I figure he's got a thing about Henry on account of growing up in that rathole.

Afternoon break, we're back at the Donut Dip. I'm feeling ticked at Benny. Let it drop, I go. But Benny never lets anything drop. Yeah, he goes, what if Henry snuck Upstairs somehow? What does that make us Reapers, if Distribution don't work right?

Next day at lunch we're back at Distribution. I'm in a crappy mood on account of tossing and turning all night thinking about what Benny said.

Foreman's just coming out. What now, he goes, still looking for your scythe? He found it, Benny goes, but then I left my wallet somewheres. Foreman looks at Benny. I can believe it, he goes.

Nice car, I go, nodding towards the New Yorker.

Suits me, he goes, climbing in.

What I don't mention is where did you get the money for a New Yorker on a Foreman's pay.

Benny keeps watch outside the office while I go through the files for what I need. When we track down the kid again, we got pictures of Henry Hubbard and Elvin McKinley.

Take a look at this, I go. Pretty easy to think McKinley was Hubbard, right?

No way, the kid goes. Look at this little birthmark on Henry Hubbard's face. Looks just like a rat. I remember it from when I was five years old and he was at the door hassling my mom for the rent when he knew the Welfare cheques weren't in yet.

Musta been tough, I go.

Guy I seen Upstairs had that birthmark, the kid goes.

There's no dealing with Benny after that. Afternoon break at the Donut Dip is more than I can take. The worst part is he's right. And we both know it.

We try the Donut of the Day, honey glaze with cream custard filling but it don't do the trick. Benny hardly touches his. I eat both. Benny's been chewing his nails again and I still got a sick feeling. If Henry Hubbard is Upstairs, where is Elvin McKinley?

I can't stop thinking about it. A guy like Elvin can't be Downstairs, it ain't right.

Three in the morning, Marion hands me my pillow and a blanket and points the way to the sofa. I'm still wide awake on the sofa when the sun comes up. But at least I know what to do.

It's risky. A lot relies on Benny and Benny's pretty spaced out.

Break time we're back at Distribution. Foreman stares at us and scratches his head. Benny shrugs his shoulders, kinda sheepish. Found my wallet, he goes, but I musta put my keys down when I was looking. Anybody seen them?

How would I know, the Foreman goes, shaking his head, don't know how a bozo like you ever made Reaper. He's still shaking his head when he climbs into the New Yorker which now has got a boat hitch with one beauty of a cruiser hooked up on it. And I think I got something figured out.

We find the kid having a smoke outside and sure enough, he's got an extra uniform. He'll drop it off tonight.

Next morning Benny's got double duty, my two snatches and his own. The delivery kid's gonna hang around the Donut Dip waiting for news and I'm on my way Downstairs in the extra uniform.

Geez, hot in here, I go when I pass the Porter. Tell me about it, he goes, not even looking up when he unloads the box and hands me back the empty. I guess if you seen one delivery guy you seen 'em all. Mind if I look around, I ask. Suit yourself, he goes, processing the paperwork. It'll keep you honest.

I spot Elvin McKinley on the fourth level, hotfootin' across a thousand miles of burning sand chasing a glass of water that keeps just out of reach. He stops to help this other guy up. The other guy grabs on to him and drags Elvin down and then just leaves him there face down in the scorching sand and takes off after Elvin's glass of water.

At least I know where he is. No way to get him out though cause the Soul Control will show him missing.

Second delivery is Upstairs. Upstairs smells nice, like baby powder. I drop off this pretty little soul and I spot Henry Hubbard sitting in this park near the entrance. Security's not too tight Upstairs. Nobody tries to break out. Henry's spread his stuff on the bench so there's no room for anyone else. He takes a little swat at a sparrow trying to land near him. Couple other guys in white are staring at him and scratching their heads.

Hey, I go, to Henry, when the Porter heads off to the can, have I got a deal for you.

What, he goes. More power, I go, make yourself a major player Upstairs.

He's interested, his nose is twitching.

Cost you though, I go, and you guys up here got no money.

I got ways, a connection, if I like what you got, he goes. Take a look, I go, special deal, won't last long. When he sticks his greedy nose in the box, I snatch him. Feels even better the second time.

The guys in white have spotted me. Illegal entry, I tell them, pointing to the box. Slipped through controls. Oh, they go, that explains it then.

I head back Downstairs. Grinning.

The Porter's staring at the Soul Control. What the hell's wrong with that thing, he goes, it's showing an extra soul down here.

I chuckle like we're buddies. Not too likely anyone would sneak in, I go.

You got that right, gotta get the friggin' technician down here again, he goes.

My first trip is to the seventh level where I dump Henry with the other scum. Then whip back up to the fourth level. Gimme a hand, buddy, I whisper to Elvin. Sure, he goes, I'll be glad t . . . He's in that box and I'm flying up that escalator two stairs at a time. I catch my breath by the Porter's station.

He's still gawking at the Soul Control. Look at that, he goes, thing's back to normal.

Maybe the humidity, I go.

At the Donut Dip, the kid from Delivery is celebrating. Elvin's on the bench in the park, I tell him, feeding the birds and chewing the fat with his new friends.

Only Benny don't look too happy, still chewing his nails.

You done great, Ben, I go, with those double snatches. Great.

Yeah but, I still got this afternoon's. It's a little girl. Car accident. And how do we know this thing won't happen again?

Don't worry about it, Benny, I go, it won't. I took care of the loose end. And I retyped your work order for the little girl.

Benny's gawking.

I grin. Twenty years typing work orders pays off.

Benny's bone-white under his cowl. I give him a pat on his shoulder. Here you go, Ben, he's all boxed up for you.

Benny gawks at the box with the Foreman's soul oozing sludge out the seams. Downstairs is stamped all over it in red.

The Sam McGee Syndrome

by Rose DeShaw

"There are strange things done

in the midnight sun by the men

who moil for gold"

Robert Service

"You have reached Professor Wilda Lauren of the University of Ottawa Department of English. Due to a personal injury, seminars on the Nineteenth Century Novel have been rescheduled . . ."

"Pick up, Willy!" My sister Janice sounded impatient. As usual. It was probably safe to answer. There should be several thousand miles between us. Janice and her schemes and dreams should be somewhere in the Yukon by now, maybe even Whitehorse.

I clicked off the rest of the message and lifted the receiver cautiously. "Janice?"

"Aunt Wilda's become a bag lady!" Ah, the new nest of hornets. A fool rushing in would find Janice there before him. "No kidding," she continued, as if I'd objected. "She looks awful. Funny hat, mismatched socks, sweaters and pants buttoned on top of each other, the whole bit."

"She's just old, Janice. Lots of people pile on the clothes in the wintertime. It's probably fifty below up there. What makes you think it's anything worse than old age?"

"It's only forty but there's a wind," she dealt with the weather first. "Aunt Wilda's on lithium for starters along with some other stuff. She's living in one of these psychiatric boarding houses. I've only met the landlady and Auntie's roommate, Alice May, a very strange woman."

I leaned back on the chesterfield, propping my left leg, the one wrapped to the thigh in plaster, on a footstool. Somewhere the strange woman's relatives were probably saying similar things about Aunt Wilda.

"Aunt Wilda pushes a shopping cart around and brings back stuff from the garbage whenever she can get through the drifts," Janice went on. "The landlady, Mrs. Lodenblatt, is a widow, dyes her hair but kind of a sweet old thing. But she draws the line at bringing any of that junk inside. So Auntie leaves the stuff behind the house and tries to sneak out for it after dark. Then Alice May tells Mrs. Lodenblatt."

"This call is costing you," I said, thinking I might become a snitch too if the alternative was living with garbage. "It sounds like Aunt Wilda's got people looking after her anyhow. She's not on the street."

Janice snorted. "Alice May makes me nervous. She's maybe six foot tall, muscles, lots of body hair. She wears bright red dresses and heavy makeup, says it's a Marilyn Monroe look. More like a lumberjack in drag. I bet she's got a criminal record or she's been to Sweden for one of those operations."

A memory of the last time I'd seen Aunt Wilda, my namesake, floated into my mind. Outside the Rideau Centre with a fresh perm and a long fur coat, holding a bunch of daffodils and laughing. Ghastly as an Ottawa winter is, we're still a long way from Yukon cold where a vindictive tundra wind slaps you silly whenever you step outside.

I remembered Aunt Wilda's sense of humor. Was this bag lady stuff some sort of elaborate joke at Janice's expense? However gullible, no one can deny my sister is good-hearted and conscientious. The Northern tour would be halted in Whitehorse till Aunt Wilda was sorted out.

The trip itself was an early Christmas gift for our folks. What they wanted most in the world, they said, was for one of us to visit the aging Northern relatives and see how things were going. First-hand reports would set their minds at ease. They themselves were getting a little past such a long trip, they quavered, trying to sound suitably aged.

As I had a broken leg at the time, not to mention gainful employment, the moving finger pretty well wrote Janice's name, which was actually the whole point of this little plot. Distance, the folks hoped, might provide some perspective on the human sponge who had moved in with Janice in the fall. I tried to be supportive but remained dubious, knowing how absence does its classic work on the heart.

Like a mindreader, Janice burbled, "I called Donny and he said Alice May might be dangerous if she finds out Aunt Wilda is worth money."

Ah, yes, Donny, the expert on everything. The unemployed vegetable who walked like a man. While a couple million other Canadians were also unemployed, Donny seemed to inhabit his own personal recession.

Janice's view of life was expressed by the classic philosophy inherent in country and western music. The brave little gal finding trouble as she fought for the love of one good man. One at a time anyhow, but at least she'd quit marrying them. Right now her happiness was rolling in the polyester arms of the ever-boyish Donald Hypchuck.

"Wish Donny was here with me," Janice said. "Though I'm sure he's taking good care of everything while I'm gone," she added wistfully, my cue to urge her to send for him. I felt like the filling in a sandwich composed of Janice and the folks, with Donny as a pickle on the side. This trip had NOT been a good idea. Janice gave a martyred sigh when she realized I wasn't coming through.

"Anyway, some sort of disability pension pays for Aunt Wilda's room," she continued. "Welfare doesn't seem to know about the jewelry she's always had in a safety deposit box at the bank. So I've been thinking. Maybe if we sold some she could get a private room at a nicer place?" This sounded like a line with a kicker at the end.

"What do Mom and Pop say?" (How typical this was. A bag lady with a fortune. The stuff newspaper headlines are made of: BAG LADY MILLION-AIRE DISCOVERED. Just the media doing their bit to make life a little more lethal for all the other bag ladies in town.)

"Oh, I'm not going to get the folks all worried about Mother's only sister living like this. You and I can handle things ourselves. The trouble is Aunt Wilda won't co-operate. She wears the key to her safety deposit box around her neck on a dirty string. And she refuses to go down to the bank with me and look at it."

"She sounds okay to me, Janice." I was getting tired of this. Crazy didn't mean stupid. "Maybe it's not fancy but she's got a bed and three meals a day. She's probably doing all right."

"Dammit, Willy. You sound like any other dumb liberal, pretending there's some sort of CHOICE involved in being a bag lady!" Oops, Janice was ticked off now.

"Did you ever think," she went on heatedly, "that if a person could CHOOSE to be a bag lady, they'd pick somewhere warmer to do it, like Florida? In our present and inadequate mental health system, nice people like Aunt Wilda end up on the streets of Whitehorse in the wintertime because when you're crazy you can't make decent choices anymore."

I gave up. The story of our life as sisters, Janice demanding and me knuckling under. "What do you want me to do?"

"Talk her into going down to the bank with me and taking out some stuff to sell. She'll listen to you."

I scribbled down the number of the boarding house and Janice's hotel, then took a deep breath and punched in the 403 area code for Whitehorse. The first call of what was probably destined to be a family telethon. My broken leg was proving a massive personal inconvenience. Everybody knew I was available to answer the phone.

"Hello?" A high-pitched voice, tense and hurried, as though a scream lay not far off. "You want who?" There was a series of muffled shouts in the background as I said I was Wilda Lauren wishing to speak to my aunt. The chainsaw came back on, identifying herself as Alice May. "Is it any warmer where you are?" she asked desperately. "It's awful here. Nothing but white, white, white," the tones rose dramatically. "At least it covers up your aunt's garbage. She has to use a shovel these days . . ."

This monologue was suddenly interrupted by heavy breathing and *oof* noises that sounded like two people arm wrestling for possession of the phone. "Oh, here's your aunt now," she said as though just noticing the recipient of the call was available.

A voice slightly out of breath said, "Willy?"

Feeling like a con artist, I explained Janice's plan about selling some jewelry to find a better place.

"I'm happy here and I'm not moving anywhere." It sounded like a decision graven in stone. "What are you REALLY trying to tell me? That my jewelry isn't safe at the bank? That it could close right down the way my parents' bank did in the depression? That something's wrong with my bank?" My aunt's voice rose a little higher at each question.

"Goodness, no! The bank's perfectly safe and so is your jewelry!" I said hastily. Aunt Wilda really did sound a little off. "We just want to be sure you're safe too."

"I see," she said in a voice that said she didn't. "Wish YOU were here," she added and hung up. Instead of Janice, bossing her around, she meant.

Janice phoned shortly afterward. "Thanks a million, Willie. She just called and agreed to go down with me in the morning. I never thought of telling her the bank might go bust. You were always the smart one in the family."

"I didn't say any such thing!" I yelped.

"Gotta go see what kind of paperwork we'll need to put together for the bank," Janice forged ahead, ignoring me as usual once the dirty work was done. "Wonder what kind of I.D. she's got?" she muttered to herself.

"Anyway, it's great to know I can get hold of you whenever I need you. I'll keep you posted." She hung up, consumed as usual with a new project.

I pottered around a bit with "Bleak House" which was on my course list next session, trying to think which of Dicken's liar characters I was most like. Even for her own good, scaring Aunt Wilda about her bank was a dirty trick. I had to tell Janice I didn't want any part of it. I called her hotel.

"What can ah do for yuh?" An unmistakable male voice. I replaced the receiver gently without replying. So Donny hadn't been able to stay away. Or maybe he'd been there all along and Janice had been trying to find a way to tell me. His presence certainly changed things as far as Aunt Wilda's situation was concerned. While I trust my sister implicitly, nothing worth money is safe around Donald Hypchuck.

Feeling fatalistic, I punched area code 403 for the third time in half an hour. "Your auntie's lying down, dearie, and I don't want to disturb the poor thing," said a reasonable but complaining voice that identified itself as Hermione Lodenblatt with an accent I couldn't place at first. "Can I take a message?"

"Yes," I said desperately. "Please tell her not to go to the bank tomorrow until she talks to me. Leave the jewelry where it is."

"All right, I've got that," the voice said. "I'll put your number here by the phone. What's that area code? Ottawa? Is it any warmer there?" Not pausing to hear my answer, her fat little voice began to boil up slowly over the line. They had ice and snow and cold that ate your heart out. "I reckon I should've known better than to leave the South and follow Lodenblatt to this godforsaken hell hole. No, no, not hell. That's way too warm..."

I interrupted her in mid-spout and hung up gently. The inmates were running the asylum.

Janice didn't have hysterics till suppertime. "Aunt Wilda's safety deposit box has been cleaned out and Donny's left me!" That last was a wail that would've brought Amnesty International leaping through any doorway.

"Are the two incidents connected?" I asked brusquely.

"What? Oh, of course not. Donny was with me the whole time," Janice said huffily. "He just flew up in case I needed help, which I did. So I took him over to meet Aunt Wilda but she wouldn't come out of her room. While I was upstairs, Donny had to sit in the kitchen and listen to Mrs. Lodenblatt talk about her arthritis," she sniffed. "Then he sat in the car while I went in the bank to check things out. The jewelry was fine then. After that we had a big fight and he took off. Oh, Willy. I don't know if I can go on without him."

On? With life? With the trip? "Pull yourself together," I snapped, "You've been through this before."

"Donny's different. He never let you see his sweetness, his thoughtfulness . . ."

The dollar signs in his eyes, I finished her sentence.

"I left this number with the bank. They just phoned and said they had a long waiting list for safe deposit boxes," Janice was explaining. "Did we want to rent it anymore now that it was empty? Yeah, can you believe it? Empty!" She repeated as though I'd been dumb enough to attempt a speaking part in this theatre of the absurd.

"Someone who looked exactly like Aunt Wilda came in about an hour after I left and took everything but it wasn't her!" Janice sniffed. "She's still in bed with a tummy upset. I don't know what I'm going to tell her tomorrow. Ah, well," she sighed. "Maybe when it gets cold enough, Donny will come back to me. He isn't used to Whitehorse."

Unless I missed my guess, Donny wasn't even IN Whitehorse anymore. Nor were Aunt Wilda's jewels. But how had he managed it if he hadn't gone into the bank? I'd better be careful of accusing him without any hard facts to go on, I reminded myself. He probably got regular infusions of cash from lawsuits for false arrest. His was a face you'd naturally pick from a line-up.

I bent a coathanger to scratch inside my cast, took a sponge bath and crawled into bed with a hot-water bottle. Ottawa winters were usually ten degrees colder than the rest of Eastern Ontario but now, with all the weather reports from Whitehorse, my nice warm campus apartment was beginning to feel like an igloo.

At 4 a.m. the phone rang. The chainsaw voice was back. I flipped on the bedside lamp, struggling awake. My little circle of light with long fingers of shadow beyond made me think of that film noir classic, "Sorry, Wrong Number", where the lone and hapless victim hears her murder plotted by phone.

"This is Alice May." Her voice had nearly found its scream. "Your number was here by the phone," it went on chattily.

Aunt Wilda's roommate. Was she drinking? "I just wanted you to know I'm taking real good care of your aunt. The heat went off and we couldn't find Mrs. Lodenblatt but she left a box of matches in the kitchen so I made a fire. I've got real big feet and they get colder than anybody else's," she rambled on while I tried to think of a response.

"My fingers were stiff as frozen fish and my nose was about to fall off but everything's all warm again. I just thought I'd let you know."

"That was a good idea, making a fire in the fireplace till the heat comes back on," I said, inanely.

"We don't have a fireplace." The line went dead.

By the time I roused the Whitehorse Fire Brigade it was too late to save the house. What had been an unsubstantial frame building with no smoke detectors or extinguishers was now a little mass of cinders under a glacier of ice where the hoses had done their work. And under that, near the furnace, the huddled body of a grey-haired woman. Poor Hermione and her yearning to be warm, I thought. But con men weren't supposed to be violent. I hoped Janice didn't go back to Donny this time.

Alice May had hightailed it to the front yard with a pair of lawn chairs under one arm and Aunt Wilda under the other, to enjoy the blaze in comfort. They were being treated for mild smoke inhalation and still occupied adjoining beds, this time in the hospital.

"They'll pull through," the fireman concluded when he called back with these details. "Funny thing, you calling us from Ottawa. Does it get real cold there?"

I mumbled a reply. Something in his report twanged my suspicions all the way up to the key of Gee Whiz! I explained my concerns to the Whitehorse police. Could someone get back to me after the autopsy? I didn't call Janice till morning. Only hysteria and recriminations would result from her rushing over to the hospital and maybe the morgue in the middle of the night. That body wasn't going anywhere.

An officer phoned with respect in his voice, shortly after five. "Good guess, ma'm. The coroner confirmed your theory immediately so we had the Vancouver police waiting at the airport. Got a confession and everything. Sometimes persons with guilty consciences panic when they see cops."

I called Janice at seven. For the first two seconds I fondly imagined that this time she wouldn't scream and yell and throw things when she heard the bad news.

Then reality set in. "Whaaaat?" She interrupted. "That poe-faced old bat was making goo-goo eyes at my Donny while I was upstairs with Aunt Wilda? Lemme get back to you, huh?" And Janice hung up.

"I'm afraid Donny's dead," I'd been trying to break it to her gently, "and Mrs. Lodenblatt . . ." But I was talking to a silent phone. Great. Hear it from strangers.

"Dammit!" Janice called about an hour later. The phone bill was going be larger than the cost of the trip. "The cops say that sticky-fingered, henna-haired old fossil knocked off my man and robbed my aunt."

We had us a country-western song here for sure.

"Alice May is a firebug," I explained. "Lodenblatt turned off the heat and left the matches out, knowing she'd use them."

"She wouldn't've had to con Donny into dressing up like Aunt Wilda," Janice said sheepishly. "He was kinda kinky like that, sometimes." The garden pests of her mind were already eating holes in her memories.

"Mrs. Lodenblatt borrows Aunt Wilda's clothes and I.D. for my sweetie," she continued bravely, "so he could sashay into the bank like a drag queen and clean out the box. Back at the house she hits him over the head and hides the body, hoping they'd think it was her?"

"Maybe she didn't know they could tell by the bones, even after a fire," I guessed. "But flames never reached that corner of the basement. Still, since firemen don't undress the victims, at least it would give her a start."

"It's colder than usual up here this winter," the police lieutenant had repeated the familiar line this morning. Perhaps it was their new motto for stirring up tourism. "Folks get the itchy foot. Can't stand it any longer so they grab everything they can get their hands on and head South. We call it 'The Sam McGee Syndrome.' After that poem by Robert Service, you know?

'The Northern lights have seen queer sights but the queerest they ever did see . . .'

"Yes, yes," I said hastily before he quoted the whole thing. I could match Service queer for queer today.

When they led Hermione Lodenblatt off in handcuffs according to the airport police, she was grinning from ear to ear. Something about how nice and warm it was in Vancouver.

"What tipped you off?" Janice asked.

"You said Mrs. Lodenblatt dyed her hair. But the body they found had gone grey."

"Poor crooked Donny," Janice sighed. "And poor Aunt Wilda. Why can't anybody understand how dangerous it is to be crazy?" But she seemed resigned to the way things had turned out.

She called back that evening to say the folks were flying in to supervise the finding of another apartment. "Mom supposes it's all for the best, given Aunt Wilda's situation. She's glad I was here to help out. I guess I should give myself more credit."

I didn't point out this was credit for setting up a situation where a lover got polished off and nearly an aunt who, without her help might've continued a lifestyle she said made her happy with Alice May and Mrs. Lodenblatt. Arson, larceny, and murder seemed to have been dormant qualities in their lives, prior to Janice.

"I'm just going to continue this trip as though Donald Hypchuck never existed," Janice declared. "After the funeral I'm flying to Inuvik."

I made supportive noises. Hanging up, I remembered which of our relatives lived in Inuvik. Uncle Pete. Strange, strange, Uncle Pete.

Ecologically Speaking (to a lawyer)

"I didn't mean to murder Jim
When I stuffed him in the garbage bin,
For when he fell and struck his head
I really thought that he was dead.

You said he was breathing when he went in,
Could you not just say I 'recycled' him?"

Joy Hewitt Mann

BIRDBRAIN

by Victoria Cameron

Had I been the only one to migrate? I'd been flying around for days before I heard a male singing, somewhere in the forest that flanked a flower-filled garden. His was a beautiful song, warm full notes over a complete range. He hit the high notes as easily as he hit the low notes.

I flitted around the trees, inspecting his territory. There was a human nest, and a birdbath, and a feeding tray scattered with seeds. He had claimed a wonderful spot. Roomy trees and flat lawn and lots of flowers around the big human nest. The whole place would be full of insects and grubs. I could sit in my nest and watch the humans, three times a day, flocked around their feeding tray on the other side of the big window, squawking at each other.

Definitely the place to raise my family. And I'd had enough of searching. It was time to get on with summer life.

He was still singing, from his secret perch. I dropped down to the birdbath, where I'd be in full view, and fluffed up my feathers. I'm pretty good looking, for a lady Northern oriole.

He must have seen me. His song reached new heights of clarity and passion. A beautiful voice, singing his own praises.

Oh, no. I hoped it wasn't *him*.

It was.

The Birdbrain.

He came swooping out of an elm tree, and there was no mistaking his brighter-than-average orange plumage. I'd seen him during migration. He stopped in a pine tree, no doubt to display his colours to best advantage against a green background. He puffed up his chest, then turned and shook his tail at me.

He saw he had my attention. I gave him the cold shoulder, just for formality's sake.

He swooped down and launched into his mating song and dance. And what a performance. He dipped. He strutted. He preened. He fluffed. He warbled. He flashed his orange rump and bumped and grinded in a shaft of sunlight. And he was good. He really was. Too good. I mean, he was the only male oriole for miles. I knew it and he knew it. But he carried on his overblown performance anyway. Talk about a birdbrain. Like I was going to turn him down if he wasn't flashy enough, when he owned the perfect garden. What choice did I have? It was mating season, he was the only male available, he had a great territory, and I had to have a mate.

So I took him.

Weeks later, I was sitting on my eggs, regretting every minute. I knew when I met him in Florida he was useless. Under Survival of the Fittest rules, he should have been hit by a truck when he paused to look at himself in the side mirror.

Here I was, hatching a clutch of eggs, watching him strut the trees and ruffle his butt when he should have been bringing home dinner. If there was no one to impress in the garden, he'd go off cruising, and come home hours after supper time with an empty beak. The Birdbrain.

When the eggs hatched, I had to get on his tail every minute, reminding him to bring home some food for the babies. I wished he was more like that robin male who stalked the lawn every day. Now there was a mate. A real hard worker. All day, every day, up and down the lawn watching for worms. Dig them up, take them home. What a guy.

Meanwhile, our nest was lurching on its foundation string and my mate was singing from the top of some tree like he hadn't a care in the world. Which he hadn't, because he was too stupid to notice anything but his own body.

By the time the babies were ready to fledge, I'd had about all I could take. Time for a face-to-face squawk about his behaviour. I looked around for his familiar orange flare in the foliage.

I spotted him, all right. Flashing at that scarlet tanager in the next tree. Wiggling his wingbars at her, practically right under my beak.

That was the last twig.

I left the kids to their argument about how far it was to fall if you stepped off the edge of the nest, and went to sit on the edge of the birdbath. I hadn't sat there since the day I selected the Birdbrain. The humans were inside, gathered around their feeding tray. They didn't notice me. I waited.

Eventually, Himself gave up on the scarlet chick, found the nest too noisy and overcrowded, and joined me on the birdbath. He went into his routine again. Fluff, strut, wiggle the butt.

The humans certainly noticed him. Mr. Bright Orange with the Big Chest. They flapped their skinny wings in our direction.

I flew off and perched in the pine tree. He followed me. I knew he liked to perch there. It was a good backdrop for his plumage, and it was within sight of the humans. It was also just far enough away for him to go from zero to sixty before he reached the birdbath.

When the humans stopped flapping, he puffed out his chest. Never could resist showing himself off to anything that moved. He spread out his orange rump and aimed at the human nest. Started his very impressive dive-bomber routine. A big sweep across the lawn, dive, bank up, show off his orange belly. Flash the humans. Blind them with brilliant orange.

He was nearly there, in full flight. I zoomed from the pine tree and swerved just short of the birdbath, flashing my less-than-brilliant plumage at him.

Just for one second, I distracted him from his flight plan. He overshot the birdbath and banked sharply. Just one second too late. Full flight.

Smash.

Right into the window.

I returned to the pine tree and sang a little song while the humans rushed out with a digging tool to bury him.

THE CLERK'S TALE

by Melanie Fogel

The air conditioning was broken again and that, along with his corns and hemorrhoids, put the desk sergeant in no mood for the old man who was approaching the counter. Short, bald and bespectacled, scrawny arms hanging from the sleeves of a flowered polyester shirt, even scrawnier legs protruding from wrinkled khaki shorts; in the sergeant's mind an image formed of a giant assembly line manufacturing little old people with little old problems for the express purpose of making his life miserable. The only thing different about this one was his walk, which wasn't so much an old man's waddle as a swagger. Swaggerers were a bigger pain than waddlers. But the old man didn't bang his fist on the counter or demand to see whoever was in charge. He just smiled in a friendly way and said, "I want to talk to somebody. I've killed my wife."

The sergeant put his hands on his hips, more to cool his armpits than express his disgust. Southern Florida had more than its share of golden-age kooks who wasted police time just trying to get some attention. And this little kook had a look of determination that told the sergeant he couldn't be dismissed to come back when it was cooler, like maybe when hell froze over.

Then the sergeant remembered Bradley. Hot-shot Bradley, who never sweated, even after his twice-weekly tennis games. Bradley, local hero and wonder boy, upstairs all alone, nursing a sprained ankle he'd self-inflicted chasing a drug pusher. The sergeant decided to make Bradley's day. He directed the little man to the detectives' room.

Bradley was not so absorbed in his paperwork that he didn't see the old man come in. He tried to guess the little guy's purpose as he made his way to the detective's desk. A missing dog? But he didn't look worried. Motorcyclists making too much noise? No, that wasn't a look of righteous outrage on his face. It was more like the look people had when they'd found out something nasty about a disliked neighbor. Bradley silently cursed the desk sergeant, whose mind he knew only too well.

"I've killed my wife, and I want to tell you about it," the old man said as he sat down.

Well, it beat statistics, and the old lady could be dead of a stroke or something. Bradley put away the monthly reports and took a multipart form out of his top drawer.

He took the man's particulars, name and address, and then asked when this murder had taken place.

"Twenty-five years ago. In Ottawa."

Bradley stopped writing. "Where's that?"

"In Canada."

The detective looked up from the form without moving his head. It was going to be a long, hot afternoon. He pulled out his bottom drawer, rested his ankle on it, and asked the old man what had happened.

"Shouldn't this be tape recorded or something?" the little man seemed disappointed. "Shouldn't there be a witness?"

"I'll hear the details first," Bradley replied, "and then we can get a formal statement from you."

The old man dabbed his forehead with a rumpled Kleenex. The perspiration was due entirely to the heat; his nerves were fine. He even smiled as he cleared his throat and then began his tale.

Marian drank, you see. We'd been married almost twenty years, and for eighteen of them she was rarely completely sober. We had one child. It was—well, it wasn't normal, and had to be institutionalized. It was the alcohol. I didn't know it at the time it was born, but when they told me later on it was like I had known it all along. It finally died. A mercy, I assure you.

We'd long ago ceased to have any kind of a social life. Anywhere Marian went she got drunk. At parties, family dinners, even a night at the theatre. Funny thing was, in all those years I never looked at other women, except to wonder what they'd be like to live with. I was faithful, not out of any sense of duty you understand, just because I didn't have—what? The moral courage? The inclination? The inclination, I guess, because when I moved down here I found a lovely woman who made me very happy. She died seven months ago—heart attack.

I thought about it for a long time. I could have divorced her, you know. We weren't Catholic or anything. But there was the insurance, and besides, I'd never done anything in my life. Anything out of the ordinary, that is. I was a clerk with the government. Never even finished college.

I first got the idea several years before, reading in the paper about an alcoholic who had died of exposure right in the heart of downtown. In a doorway, during a blizzard. It only took overnight. He'd just fallen asleep in the snow and not woken up. At the time I thought what a nice way to go, and considered it for myself. As I said, it wasn't a very happy marriage.

But Marian spent more and more of her time dead drunk, and she couldn't remember what had happened when she woke up, and I thought if I tried to kill her by putting her out in the cold overnight and failed, she wouldn't remember it anyway, so I might as well try.

Once I'd made up my mind to do it, it was an awful wait for the right weather. And winter came late that year, so it was a couple of weeks before Christmas. I can still hear the radio announcer's voice: "Rain starting about four o'clock, changing to snow about eight." They were predicting ten inches. The only thing that could go wrong was that the rain wouldn't change to snow, in which case Marian would spend another night in a drunken stupor and I'd spend another night watching TV. And I'd have to try again.

To my joy I drove home in misting rain that was getting colder by the second. I took the two bottles of rye that I'd had in the trunk since November and carried them into the house.

When Marian saw me with the liquor bags she asked, "Is it my birthday?" She was still in her nightgown and housecoat. She never got dressed any more unless she had to go out to buy liquor. She was already tipsy, like she usually was at that time of day.

"No," I told her. "I've just decided if you can't beat them, join them. We're both going to get drunk tonight."

She was sceptical. But I poured us both a drink from one of the new bottles and I had a sip first. Then she toasted my "reformation."

By eight o'clock the snow was beginning to collect on the window sill and Marian was unconscious on the sofa. I poured a little extra rye down her throat to make sure. Then I tried to pick her up.

Marian wasn't a big woman, but she was heavier than I'd expected. Of course she was a dead weight, and I'd never bothered to keep in shape; there didn't seem to be any need. It certainly didn't make any difference to Marian. I tried to sling her over my shoulder like I'd seen in the movies, but I couldn't manage it and finally ended up dragging her to the kitchen. I laid her on the floor to open the back doors, screen door and outside door. The screen door closed automatically so I had to hold it open with the first thing handy—a carton of milk from the fridge. The snow blew into the kitchen and wet the floor. The cold air was invigorating. The wind, which

I could hear more than feel in the shelter of the kitchen, churned the snow so that it seemed to be falling up.

Our yard had a high fence, but I checked all the neighboring second-storey windows I could see just to make sure I wouldn't be spotted. All the drapes and curtains were closed snug against the weather. I was never one much for gardening. It's an expensive proposition, and most of my extra money went for Marian's booze. So the yard was just weeds and patches of bare earth, with a stubborn lilac bush by the back porch. The snow was still melting as it hit the ground; the earth wasn't frozen yet. That worried me, because maybe it wouldn't get cold enough. But I figured that the worst that could happen would be Marian would wake up in the yard and not know how she got there. I could use the excuse she must have wandered out there while she was drunk and I was asleep. It was the excuse I had planned to use when they found the body. In fact, setting a precedent might be a good idea. This was running through my mind as I took her under the shoulders to drag her out into the yard.

Just in time I realized that if I dragged her, her heels might show traces, and I couldn't risk that. So I sat on a kitchen chair, and kind of pulled her up slowly by her armpits, until I had her by the waist. I stood up and she immediately flopped over. I braced myself against the kitchen table and hefted her around so she faced me. Her head lolled against my shoulder and I could feel her slobbering down my neck. With one arm around her waist and the other under her buttocks I stepped outside.

I carried her towards the opposite end of the yard. The wind was wicked: sharp, cold, and wet. Marian kept my chest warm, but my back and arms were freezing. She kept slipping because both her nightgown and her housecoat were made of that soft, slithery stuff women like to wear. The wind cut right through my shirt, icing the sweat I'd built up trying to lift Marian. I realized I should have put on a coat and boots, but it was too late now. What was even worse was the snow on my glasses blurring my vision. Luckily, there was nothing in front of me to trip over. But I had to stop after every three steps and hoist her back into place. It took a long time to walk thirty feet.

I put her down by the far left corner of the fence, because the wind was blowing that way. The snow would pile up there, you see. I guess you've never seen a snowdrift. As soon as I stood up again I stopped sweating and felt my wet shirt freezing to my ribcage. I ran back to the house and collapsed on the kitchen chair.

I sat there, panting, frozen and exhausted, while my glasses steamed up. I placed them on the table and took deep breaths to recover. When I put them on again, I noticed to my horror that I'd tracked mud into the house. I turned on the porch light and went outside again, and I saw that I'd left footprints—my footprints, in a deep, erratic line leading right up to Marian's body and a shallower, straight line leading back to the house.

For a moment I was paralysed. In all that planning, I'd never thought of footprints. Footprints are evidence, aren't they? Plaster casts and all that? I kicked off my soggy, muddy shoes as if they were responsible for the accusing finger I saw pointing at me. Then I wondered what to do.

My first impulse was to bring her back into the house and forget the whole thing. But it had taken me so long to make up my mind, to resolve to do it. And it was too good a plan, I couldn't abandon it completely. I thought of waiting till the ground was frozen, but by then there'd be snow on it so I'd still be leaving footprints. Then it hit me that Marian's footprints were the ones that should be there, not mine, and I wondered if I could just get rid of mine and let people—the police, I guess—assume that the ground had been frozen when she went out there. But her body was muddy. Would they think her body heat had melted the ground? I couldn't take that chance. I'd lived all my life in Canada but I knew nothing about soil temperatures or how to read footprints in the snow or anything like that. I was a clerk, after all. So I couldn't take the chance that nobody would notice Marian hadn't left footprints. What to do?

I thought maybe I could carry her with her back to me, even if she did flop over, and then sort of "walk" her back to that spot by the fence. If I kept my legs wide apart, my footprints would be outside hers and I could erase them somehow. But how? I went to the front vestibule, where we kept a shovel for the front walk and I always left my overshoes. I put on my overshoes and took the shovel back with me. When I went into the yard again I saw the snow was just starting to stick to the earth. I dragged the back of the shovel over the nearest footprints and found I could erase them that way. But I had to work quickly, while the ground was still soft and the snow was still melting.

I ran up to Marian, hoisted her up (she was even heavier) and carried her back to the porch. Again I'd forgotten to put on a coat, but there wasn't time, not a second to spare. There was no way I could retrace my path while carrying her, so I had to wipe out every mark I'd made, to make sure there'd be clear ground for her feet to land on.

Marian lay on the porch this whole time, dead to the world. I don't know what I would have done if she'd woken up. Smashed her head in with the shovel? I doubt it. I didn't want to hurt her. Just have her fall asleep and not wake up. She'd made my life miserable, but twenty years of living with someone creates a bond of some kind. I didn't want to hurt her.

What with the cold and the bending and the carrying, my back was starting to ache. I tried to straighten up to get the cramp out, but standing straight up in the wind was worse than bending over. At last I'd wiped out every trace of my footprints and I was back at the porch and hoping my arms had enough strength left to carry Marian one more time.

She was wearing fuzzy slippers. Big, wide, soft fuzzy slippers. Would fuzzy slippers leave footprints? Did it matter, so long as they got muddy? I couldn't put shoes on her, not unless I put clothes on her too, because it wouldn't make sense. Overshoes? Would a drunk woman deciding on a stroll in a back yard in the middle of a blizzard think to put on overshoes? Wouldn't she also put on a coat? And a hat and gloves and a scarf—no, I couldn't face doing all that. Besides, if she were that warmly dressed she might survive.

I think I was a little drunk myself. Not on liquor, on adrenalin. I know I wasn't thinking as clearly as usual. I remember looking across that black expanse of yard, that howling wind, thoughts churning in my mind like the snow falling up. "Don't take any chances," I told myself. "You don't know enough to take chances."

I tried to lift her into position but couldn't do it there on the porch. I dragged her back into the house and sat on the chair again. The screen door had started to slip closed so I kicked the milk carton back into place. As I started to lift her she vomited, only a little, and most of it landed on her. Good. Maybe she'd vomit some more and choke on it.

By locking my arms under her breasts I could carry her with her feet about half an inch off the ground. Her head fell forward but not the rest of her. I prayed to God she wouldn't vomit then.

I reached the screen door just as it slammed shut. I started to cry. Why, oh why was everything going against me? What gods were protecting this drunken, slatternly woman and wouldn't help me? I got angry at them, and determined not to let them win. I put Marian down, gently so there wouldn't be bruises, propped the screen door open with another kitchen chair under its handle, and sat down to lift Marian again.

What a sight we must have made! Forgive my chuckling, I can laugh about it now but let me tell you, it was hell at the time. Not the worst night of my life, though. Does that surprise you? Well, it wasn't. There were lots worse nights than that. Nights when I had to make excuses for my drunken wife and play the stoic. Nights when I had to face the pity of friends and family. Nights when I wondered what life would have been like with a sober woman.

I was never an ambitious man. All I ever wanted from life was a home and a family. I would have been a good husband and a good father if I'd been given the chance. I know I would have. I was a steady worker, moderate in my habits and even-tempered. But Marian had robbed me of the chance to be a husband and father. I wanted so little, but the bi—. But she denied me even that.

So there I was, with my right hand grasping my left wrist, walking with my legs as far apart as I could, with Marian's legs hanging straight down, my arms trembling from cold and strain, struggling with her slippery, sodden weight. For each step I took I lowered Marian, first on the left side, then on the right side. Her knees would bend and mine were on the verge of buckling, the whole time the wind blowing snow on my face and glasses, the melting snow trickling down my forehead and into my eyes.

Sightless, my arms threatening to pull out of their sockets, I made it to the far corner of the yard. I bent to lay Marian down and my glasses slipped off. In my natural blindness and the blinding dark I couldn't find them. I ran back to the house to get a flashlight along with the shovel. The ground felt harder, somehow. Was it freezing yet?

Have you ever tried to find a flashlight when you really need one? I couldn't remember the last time I'd used it. Had no idea where it was. Marian wasn't the kind of person who had a place for everything and everything in its place and, frankly, neither was I.

I finally found it in the hall closet, having torn out several drawers in the meantime. The batteries worked, at least that was going in my favor. I ran back into the yard, keeping my legs wide apart so as not to create any new footprints, to find my glasses.

Another piece of good luck, I hadn't laid Marian down on them. Nor were they broken. I wiped them with my shirt tail and put them on. I used the flashlight to check that Marian was lying in a natural position, and that her slippers were properly muddied.

She'd lost a slipper. Why hadn't I seen it while I was crossing the yard? What if I had stepped on it? I looked all over the yard, twisting my body so I could stay in one spot and not make any more footprints. But nothing has color in the middle of the night in the middle of a snowstorm, and what with the tufts of weed and the occasional rock that littered the yard, I couldn't make it out.

I shone the flashlight on Marian's bare foot. It was muddy. I started to wipe the mud off but it smeared so I stopped. Could a drunk woman lose a slipper and not notice it? My own hands had long since gone numb. Yes, she could, I decided, so as long as the slipper was lying in her tracks I'd be all right. I got down on my hands and knees, all wide apart so as not to mark Marian's footprints, and beetle-like searched for the slipper.

My shirt worked its way out of my trousers and the wind lifted it from my exposed back. Snow fell on my kidneys and tickled my spine. I crawled until I found the slipper, lying on its side near the porch.

I had to make a decision. Remove the other slipper and try to muddy Marian's other foot, or try to clean her foot and put the slipper back on, or leave things as they were, maybe moving the slipper closer to where she lay. I tried to think like a policeman. What evidence would the slippers and footprints reveal? I crawled back to Marian, examining her footprints as I went.

They were very faint, just slight impressions, much slighter than mine, although that was by the weak light of the flashlight. Would they show up more distinctly under the light of the sun? And I couldn't make out any difference between them. Her toes hadn't left any marks the slippered foot didn't. But when I got back to her I saw that the slipper she had on was definitely much muddier; much, much dirtier than the bare foot. More than could be accounted for by one foot having been shod for a short time. Had I unconsciously lowered one foot more heavily than the other? There was no time to think about it. And I certainly wasn't going to start all over again.

I straddled back to the slipper by the porch. There was hardly any mud on its sole. I put my hand in it and "stepped" it into some of my footprints, which I'd have to smooth out anyway. It was so warm! That, I think, is my clearest memory, of how warm my hand felt when I put that slipper on. Then I laid the slipper closer to the body. I put it on its side, at the angle I'd found it, hoping that was the natural way it would have come off. Then with the flashlight in one hand and the shovel in the other I smoothed out all my footprints, working my way backwards towards the house. I had to stop every few seconds to wipe snow from my glasses. My nose ran so badly I had to breathe through my mouth, every gasp freezing the nerves in my teeth. The cold entered by my ears and shot pain from my eardrums into my throat. Floridians don't realize how painful cold can be, especially when it's inside you. The flashlight died before I'd finished, but by that point I was close enough to the house to see by the porch light, and that's how I finished the job.

In the kitchen, I tore off my wet, filthy clothes, and headed for a hot tub. I hurt all over, but it was the pain in my head that was unbearable. Every extremity except my toes, which had been booted, stung as if swollen with venom. My back was stiffened with cramp and my arms and legs ached from the weight they'd carried. My nose ran uncontrollably, although I couldn't feel it at all except when the liquid reached my mouth. I was terrified I'd got frostbite. I looked at myself in the bathroom mirror, which kept steaming up, but I couldn't see any white patches, so I figured I was all right. Sliding into the hot water was agony.

You'd think after what I'd just been through, with all that adrenalin flowing and my mind focused on what I might have overlooked, that I couldn't sleep at all. But I did, like a baby, with no dreams whatsoever. When I woke it was light, and I was choking.

I knew even before I opened my eyes that I had a terrible cold and any muscle I might move would torture me. I recalled the previous night instantly. My mind was clear, and I knew exactly what I would do.

I got up slowly to minimize the pain. I looked through the bedroom window out onto the back yard, which was smoothly covered in snow. There was a definite rise in the far left corner, but nothing that the wind wouldn't account for. My cold was the perfect excuse for calling in sick, which I did, and then went downstairs to make myself breakfast.

There was mud all over the floors, and my clothes still lay in a wet heap in the kitchen. The chair still held back the screen door. Drawers and cupboards hung open, their contents ransacked. For a moment I couldn't remember why I had made such a mess. Then I did remember, and I didn't see the flashlight. I panicked, thinking I'd left it in the yard, until I found it in my trousers pocket. Burning with fever and with every joint and muscle screaming in protest, I cleaned up the kitchen, and the rest of the house, except for the empty rye bottles in the living room. I made it all brighter and tidier than Marian ever did, and then I boiled an egg and made some toast which I ate in bed.

Just before noon I called the police to say my wife was missing. They weren't very interested. They told me I had to wait twenty-four hours, and then I should come down to the station. I explained about my cold, which the man could certainly hear over the phone, but he wasn't even sympathetic about that. Well, what could I do? I had to wait.

I waited three days before I called again. I still had the cold, and they still insisted I come to the station. I asked if they could at least, please, check all the hospitals, surely they had some kind of routine for that? That evening they called to say she wasn't dead or injured. I knew better.

So then I had to think, should I discover the body myself? It would give me a nice Christmas present. But how? Why would I be shoveling the snow in the back yard? Yet I was too impatient to wait until spring.

Finally, because more snow was predicted, I went down to the police station to make out a formal missing persons report.

They asked me routine questions. No, I didn't have a recent picture of her. No, I didn't check with any of her friends because she doesn't have any friends. She drinks, you see. Why didn't I look to see if she packed a bag? Why didn't I notice if any of her clothes were gone? Well, I've had this terrible head cold, I haven't been thinking straight. What did I think happened to her? Well, anything could have happened to her. She drinks. She was drunk that night. I went to bed early because of my cold and when I woke up she wasn't there. They agreed to send someone around to my house.

I don't know why the policeman decided to walk around the back yard. The rise in the far left corner wasn't that noticeable. But he did, and he found her. He was very sympathetic.

It went so well I could hardly believe it. They never even looked for the other slipper, let alone footprints. Ha! Even the insurance company paid without a peep. I stayed at my job until the autumn, and then I decided to retire down here.

 — — — — — —

Bradley look hard into the little man's bright blue eyes. They were positively twinkling. And his lips were struggling against a smirk. "Why are you confessing all this now?" he asked.

"Confessing?" the old man repeated. "Yes, I guess it is a confession, although my conscience has never bothered me about it." At this point the smirk won.

"I'm dying, you see. The big C. So it doesn't matter now if anybody knows. Why am I confessing? Well, it's like this: killing Marian, and getting away with it, is the only big thing I've ever done in my whole life. The only extraordinary thing. And I guess I just wanted to tell somebody about it. To boast, if you like."

The little man stood up and started out of the room. His shoulders held high, there was more than a hint of pride in his step. At the door, he turned and smiled at Bradley. More than a smile. The little man was gloating.

Malice Domestic

There's sure to be some violence
When husbands kill their wives.
There's sure to be some mayhem
With fists and guns and knives.
But there's likely to be poison
As silent as a mouse,
That won't show up in autopsy
When a wife knocks off her spouse.

Joy Hewitt Mann

LAUNDRESS FANTASTIQUE

by Elizabeth Syme

This is not a story I would tell everyone. I'm not saying this to impress you. It's just that some people think so logically. That kind would think me a bit of a weirdo if I were to tell them what I'm about to tell you now.

I remember the day it began because it was the day on which the new National Gallery of Canada was officially opened. It was towards the end of May, when the lilacs were in bloom in Ottawa. The opening was a black-tie affair with the governor general and the prime minister and all the beau monde of Ottawa in attendance. The gallery opened with that wonderful Degas Exhibition. I'm sure you remember it.

Anyway, I had been trying to find a new cleaning lady. Someone to come in once a week and clean the apartment. I live on Wurtemburg Street, in a large apartment building. Quite a classy place, in fact. I had telephoned an employment agency and they said they would send someone to see me.

Well, that's how it happened. I was walking up the driveway to the apartment on that Friday evening when I noticed a woman looking rather lost in a semi-detached kind of way that made me feel I owed it to myself to try to assist her. She looked elderly, but when I spoke to her and saw her face more clearly, I realized she was one of these people who might be any age, any nationality, and even any sex. It's difficult to explain, suffice it to say I know an indeterminate person when I meet one.

"Are you looking for anyone or any place in particular?" I asked.

She turned her large sombre eyes on me. "I'm looking for a place to work."

She spoke with a French accent and had difficulty with her English pronunciation. She was dressed in a long, old-fashioned black coat. Her hair was mid-brown and dressed in a kind of Gibson-girl style. As I was saying, I was expecting someone from the employment agency to do my laundry and cleaning. I should also tell you I'm famous for jumping the gun; so, true to type, I jumped right in.

"You wouldn't be from the employment agency by any chance? Are you looking for Katherine Reilly?"

She looked at me in a puzzled way. Perhaps it was my imagination, but she seemed to have a kind of wistful expression on her face. I'm a sucker for wistful expressions.

"I'm looking for a cleaning lady. Someone to clean and do some laundry," I added.

"Laundry?" She said the word in a kind of way that made me feel she sensed the meaning of the word rather than understood it.

"Blanchisserie."

Her face lit up. "Blanchisserie! That is what I want to do. I will work for you? No?"

I opened my purse, took out my notebook, and wrote my apartment and telephone number. "Come and see me on Monday morning at nine o'clock."

As you can see, I make quick decisions and act on them equally quickly. I'm well known for this in my family.

"By the way, what's your name?"

She hesitated. "Mathilde. . . Mathilde Pauphilat." It was as if she didn't say her name very often.

"Okay, Mathilde, I'll expect you on Monday."

Well, to speed things up a bit, Mathilde did come on Monday morning. In fact, she came every Monday morning for the next twelve weeks. She cleaned the apartment and she did the laundry and ironing. And such laundry and ironing! She starched, ironed and sewed! My husband's shirts were laundered to perfection. My blouses had never been so creaseless. Pillowcases, sheets, curtains, Mathilde laundered them with love. She almost caressed them as she worked. And she adored my two steam irons! I had to explain how they worked at first. But after she had mastered them, there was no stopping her!

Now is the time to explain to you that Mathilde was not everyone's cup of tea. She was taciturn and not much given to small talk. I put the latter down to her not being too comfortable communicating in English. On her second Monday, I offered her a glass of calvados. Did she know what to do with that! So I took to offering her a glass every Monday when she arrived.

Now, here is what all this is leading up to. My husband and I had not yet visited the new National Gallery of Canada or the Degas Exhibition.

Some friends had tickets which they were unable to use, so they very kindly passed them on to us.

I remember, it was a beautiful summer evening. We arrived at the National Gallery and joined the line-up to get into the Degas Exhibition. The paintings and the sculptures were wonderful. I seem to remember we had just gone into gallery number five when we came to that painting!

Perhaps you know the one I mean? The one with the laundresses?

As I walked towards it, I had the strangest feeling someone was looking at me with a lot of intensity, and this was coming from the painting. I looked at the laundress on the left. Well, who do you think it was?

Mathilde!

I'm not kidding you! It was our Mathilde!

I can tell you, I was very scared. But I can, when the occasion warrants it, be quite gutsy, so I walked forward and looked into her face. The dark eyes stared back at me. Not a sign of recognition.

My husband frowned at me. "Is anything the matter?"

"Don't you see who it is?"

"No, I don't. What are you talking about?"

"It's Mathilde."

"You're crazy." He gave me a not-so-gentle push that took us to the next painting.

I looked back over my shoulder, and there were Mathilde's dark eyes following me. There was even a little smile hovering on her lips. I gave her a "wait till I see you next time" look, and turned away.

Next Monday, what do you think? There was a gentle tap at the door and Mathilde stood there, large as life.

I had no clear plan as to what I was going to say. I intended to wait to see how she was going to treat the situation. She walked in, took off her coat, and hung it up in the cupboard. She gave me a curt bonjour and walked into the kitchen.

I decided to play it cool. I have always agreed with the dictum "If you can't beat them, join them." I went to the buffet, got the bottle of calvados, and took it into the kitchen. Mathilde's eyes brightened when she saw the bottle. I poured a substantial amount into the glass and handed it to her. She raised it to her nose and sniffed it. She took a deep breath and inhaled it more fully. She had a habit of closing her eyes as she went through this Monday morning ritual. I suppose that, when you are a part of canvas and paint, alcohol has that kind of effect on you.

Of course, I tried to trap her. I laid all kinds of snares. I asked her about paintings. Was she fond of sculptures? Her expression remained impassive, and she would give a slight shrug. A resigned look would appear on her face. For some reason, after my visit to the Degas Exhibition, a bond began to grow between us. You might even call it a conspiracy of silence.

It occurred to me that the National Gallery of Canada was always closed to the public on Mondays. Was this why Mathilde was able to come and work for me? I wondered if there was an empty space in the Degas painting. I would have given anything to have been able to go and look at it, just to see if Mathilde had actually vacated the space she always occupied.

I ought to explain that, at this time, Mathilde's skills as a laundress became even greater. She laundered everything in the apartment she could lay hands on. She washed rugs, cushions, bed covers, velvet curtains, with an expertise that has, to my knowledge, never been surpassed. I had taken to giving her a second glass of calvados shortly before lunch. It fascinated me the way she sat, cradling it in her hands, and then taking a sip and letting the tip of her tongue run gently round her lips.

Her other love was my smaller steam iron. She would polish and clean it until it shone. When she measured water into it, it was like a religious rite. She would stand at the ironing board and pick it up and gaze at it as if it were a pearl beyond price.

I tried to speak to my husband about this but, as the weeks went by, I gave up. My husband is a scientist with the National Research Council of Canada. Everything has to be explained in scientific terms. I'm sure you know what I mean.

In rather a bizarre way, Mathilde and I enjoyed each other's company. It was not that we came to understand one another any better. It was just that we became more comfortable with each other.

Anyway, it was just before the Degas Exhibition closed at the National Gallery of Canada, at the end of August. Mathilde came that last Monday and, as usual, got set into her work.

It's funny, the way you get premonitions. I always feel I get more than my share of them. I had a kind of sad, empty feeling inside me, so I poured myself a glass of calvados when I poured Mathilde hers. She sat, as usual, cradling her glass, which she savoured to the full. When she drained the last drop, she closed her eyes. I could see that she held it in her mouth for a long time, before she let it slip over her throat.

She stood up and went to the cupboard to get her coat. As she opened the apartment door to let herself out, she turned and made the longest speech she had ever made to me.

"Au revoir, madame. Je vous remercie beaucoup de votre gentillesse. Je ne vous oublierai jamais."

I looked at her and nodded mutely. I found I had a lump in my throat. I've always been oversensitive to such occasions.

You are wondering what happened? I'll tell you. The Degas Exhibition closed the following Saturday. The next Monday, I waited for Mathilde's arrival. Of course, she didn't come. I felt desolate and sad. The apartment seemed so empty and chilly. I went to the buffet to get the calvados. I knew we had a full bottle of the stuff.

It was gone!

I'm not one to tell a lie about something like this.

Suddenly, a thought struck me and I went over to the cupboard where I keep my steam irons. Yes, you've guessed correctly. The smaller one that Mathilde had loved, cleaned, and polished had disappeared.

I confess I was utterly taken aback and, having no longer any calvados, I poured myself a large glass of Irish whiskey.

I have not told anyone about this. That's really why I'm confiding in you now. You seem to be the kind who would understand such a story. You are wondering about the Degas Exhibition? It went to Vancouver and to New York before returning to France. I bought the Vancouver newspapers and also the New York newspapers. In all the reviews of the exhibition, there was never a mention that the laundress on the left side of the Degas masterpiece had taken to using a small steam iron.

However, Mathilde is not going to get the better of Katherine Reilly. I have done my research and know the painting is owned by people who live in a small chateau in the Loire Valley. Next summer, my husband and I plan to vacation in France. I know the chateau is open to the public, and I intend to go and look at the painting.

I plan to buy the largest bottle of calvados I can find. I will stand in front of the painting and offer it to Mathilde. I know she will not be able to resist it.

But before I give it to her, I shall ask her to return my small steam iron.

DEATH AT
NETWORK NEWS

by Marguerite McDonald

The kitchen helper began fumbling for his cigarettes as he hurried out the delivery door of the National Press Building. It had been a hectic and harried evening for the little Chinese man, and his whole body longed for a smoke. Song Ji had exactly five minutes for his break; he intended to savour every second of it. He selected a cigarette and noticed he had only one more left.

At that moment, a body came hurtling down through the September twilight. It smacked the pavement beside him with a loud and terrible sickening sound.

Song Ji recoiled and dropped his cigarette package. He huddled against the wall for a moment and then he forced himself to look at the broken mass. There was no sound, no movement. It was a man—a very dead man.

Song Ji retreated to the delivery door. He knew he should go for help, but then someone would call the police. Back home in China the police meant big trouble. In this new country, . . . no, he couldn't risk it.

He looked back into the gathering darkness one more time. Then he stumbled through the door into the light and safety of the kitchen inside.

Upstairs on the eighth floor of the National Press Building, Maude Wilkinson kicked the wall of her editing booth and swore. Her editor, George Cromwell, ejected a video cassette and Maude slapped another into his outstretched hand. "We'll try two more tapes," she said. "If we don't find that clip we'll have to drop it."

"I thought you said it was essential," he objected.

"I said we'll skip it . . . We're running out of time."

Maude could hear ringing telephones and the jerky intense voices of people under pressure all around her in the network's Ottawa bureau. She glanced at the clock. Eight minutes to eight. Sixty-eight minutes until they went live to the network with the television special.

Tension was locking up the back of her neck. She tried rotating her shoulders and stretching her long body—but nothing helped. She was straining toward the video monitor as she watched images flash by in fast forward. She had to find that clip! In a few minutes other reporters would start screaming at her to get out of the editing booth and give them a turn.

The tape came to an end and Maude swore again as her editor jammed another cassette into the machine.

She noticed Amir Aziz in the next booth. "Amir," she shouted, "you shot this stuff at the P.M.'s cottage. Do you remember him talking about his family? You know, sickness and health, blah, blah, blah."

The cameraman came to her door and squeezed into the booth. "It's right after the shots of the grandchildren in the water." His voice was tight, his body rigid. Maude glanced at him sharply: she could tell something was upsetting him but there was no time to pursue it.

He stood beside her a moment, obviously waiting to see them locate the clip—but then he checked the clock. "I've got to go. Victor Bloody Todd is doing a promo live into the network at the top of the hour. And we've got to do a good job framing our anchor's precious curly head."

It was exactly five to eight. Maude could feel the loud beat of her heart as George laid the clip into place. Just two more sequences and she'd be done. All except her on-camera.

She became aware that Amir was paging Victor Todd. Then a producer from the specials unit began paging him too.

George continued to lay their shots on the voice track, but Maude's eyes kept darting to the off-air monitor where the network's anchor was supposed to appear.

Victor Todd's image did not materialize. Instead, the face of Jessica Winchley, the specials unit's feature reporter, came up on the screen. George punched up the off-air sound.

All over the floor, silence fell abruptly. Everyone stood transfixed as a cool Jessica ad-libbed her way through the highlights of the special to come. It was a flawless performance but Maude could tell Jessica was rattled under that surface composure.

Frank Desroches, the Ottawa bureau chief, exploded out of the master control area. "WHERE THE HELL IS VICTOR? WHO SCREWED UP?" He grabbed one of the producers. "WHAT THE HELL DID YOU DO WITH YOUR FUCKING STAR?"

Maude reached back and eased the sliding door closed, but the glass couldn't shut off the chaos outside.

Something had gone seriously wrong. Victor Todd might be a toad in human form—but he was a pro. He didn't just forget to turn up for a network spot.

Ten minutes later, George Cromwell began laying in the last sequence.

Maude grabbed her purse and script, and rushed to meet her camera crew at the elevator doors. She'd have them shoot out on the sidewalk, in that spot near the corner of the building. It wasn't ideal but it was fast. She shrugged. Tonight, fast was best. And they could frame the shot with Parliament's East Block in the background.

While the crew set up, she dug out a mirror and checked her make-up under the streetlight. She began to apply fresh lipstick.

A muscle car slowed down in the curb lane. Maude groaned. Oh, no! Yahoos. Not tonight! What was there about television crews that attracted yahoos? Two guys in baseball caps leaned out the windows beside the camera and shouted "Hi, Mom!" and then the driver gunned the motor and the car screeched away.

The tube of lip colour slipped from Maude's fingers and rolled down the driveway beside the building. She darted after it into the shadows—and tripped over a form splayed out in the darkness.

Maude rolled away from the moist, disgusting object and shouted at the crew to bring their light. The camera's lamp revealed the horror she'd stumbled across: a mass of blood and flesh and bone. She'd sprawled over what remained of an arm and a leg.

In the midst of the terrible mess, she could see a shock of curly, black hair. It was the unmistakable permed hair of Victor Todd.

Maude wanted to curl herself into a ball. She wanted to cover her face with her hands and rock back and forth. She wanted to moan "No! No! No! No! No!" over and over again.

Instead, the reporter in Maude raced to the doors of the National Press Building, and yelled at the security guard to call the police. She retrieved her lipstick—and finished her make-up with a steady hand. She took off her blood-stained jacket: she'd do the on-camera in her shirt-sleeves.

Somehow, she got through her lines to camera on the first take. Then she picked up the auxiliary light and walked back down the driveway with the crew, to shoot the body and the scene around it, before the police arrived.

It was a few moments later that Maude found herself clutching her jacket against her chest, shaking violently in the cool September air, as the first police car drew to a halt beside her.

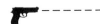

Just having a scotch in her hand made Maude feel better. Frank Desroches kept a bottle in his bottom drawer—and the bureau chief poured her a generous amount. By the time Staff-Sergeant Jamieson came to interview her, Maude had regained some of her composure. She was slumped in one of Frank's office chairs, with his large coat wrapped around her, staring at the special on the office monitor.

As bureau chief, Frank insisted on staying with her.

"Miss Wilkinson," the staff sergeant said, "Do you know why Mr. Todd was sitting on a window-sill here on the eighth floor?"

"I can tell you that, Staff Sergeant," Frank interjected. "I had that special window installed so we can shoot our reporters in bad weather. It swings open and we can frame them with Parliament Hill behind. They're inside, but there's a sense of place, and you get the distant noise from the street. It gives the story more immediacy and texture."

The staff sergeant shot Frank a cold look, turned his back on him, and fixed his eye on Maude. "But, MISS WILKINSON, it wasn't raining tonight," he observed.

Maude nodded. "Right, Staff Sergeant, but they were doing the promo live into the network. If they'd shot it outside they'd have had to lay cables or set up a dish. It wasn't worth it: they're doing the special itself from the studio upstairs. Anyway, they didn't have time. The prime minister dropped his bombshell at three o'clock. They barely had time to fly Victor and the Specials Unit in from Toronto. All of us here in the bureau were scrambling to make the deadline."

"Now, Miss Wilkinson, do you know anyone with a grudge against Mr. Todd? Anyone who'd want to hurt him?"

Maude and Frank's eyes met. In spite of herself, Maude snorted. "Don't ask who bore him a grudge," she said. "Ask who didn't. It's difficult to explain how someone who was so lovable on air could be so loathsome in real life, but he was a jerk. A jerk with power."

A uniformed policeman knocked. The staff sergeant was needed down below in the driveway. "I'll be back," he said.

Maude and Frank watched more of the special without speaking. Now that it was actually on the air, Frank's work for the special was over. He poured himself a scotch and sat back in his chair, but he clearly wanted to talk about Victor Todd. "It's hard to believe I actually helped that s.o.b. get ahead in this organization. I know he's dead, but the nicest thing I can say about him is that he was an offensive, arrogant bastard! And ever since last spring . . .

Maude bit her lip to keep from smiling. She remembered the blow-up between Frank and Victor during the spring election campaign. Even by network standards, it had been a major confrontation: two large men, standing toe to toe, screaming into each other's faces.

"You hear what happened at the planning meeting at seven?" Frank asked.

"I heard there was trouble."

Frank lit a cigar and began puffing energetically. "He decided he didn't want Jessica doing any feature interviews for the special. He'd do all the live interviews himself. It was crazy. Jessica's the business expert. She's a natural to do the economic impact stuff. When he didn't get his way, he picked up a phone and called the president."

Maude was incredulous. "The president?"

Frank nodded. "Yeah. The great leader himself. At home."

Then he lowered his voice, imitating the anchor's deep range. "Look, fellah, I'm sick and tired of women with no talent getting slots on my show just because they're women. I want a little respect around here. The way I see it, that American network offer is looking better and better all the time. You get a lot of respect at a million bucks a year."

Frank Desroches looked sadly at his cigar. "And guess what? The president bought it. And everyone swallowed hard and said, 'Ready, aye, ready, sir.'"

"Including you."

"Including me. I like my job. But after the meeting broke up, I told The Toad exactly what I thought of him."

"I could hear you ranting at him when I came back to my desk to pick up some notes."

"I never rant."

"Yeah, right." Maude grinned affectionately at the large rumpled man with his feet on the desk. He was such a teddy bear! A very big, moth-eaten teddy bear—six-feet-four, balding, and paunchy—a teddy bear with a touch of the grizzly when aroused.

Sometime after the special and the network news that followed, Maude was amazed to find that Jessica Winchley was still in the office. She was sitting in a screening booth, analyzing a tape of the special. She rewound a section, played it again—and made a couple of notes. She was totally focussed on the screen.

Finally Jessica looked up, brushed her blond hair out of her eyes, and smiled wearily at Maude.

"You were simply stunning on the special," Maude told her. "You must be very pleased."

"I'm always better under pressure," Jessica laughed. "Crazy, isn't it?" Then her expression darkened. "You know, I wanted a chance like this so badly. I've worked and worked and worked. But I didn't want to get it this way. It's horrible to think of Victor lying there on the pavement just below us . . . even if he was a bastard."

"I hear he was particularly obnoxious at the final planning meeting."

"Do you know what he said to me after it broke up? He said, 'Sorry about that phone call to the president, Jessie baby, but it had to be done. I figure anyone who's slept her way to the top the way you have—a girl like you—well, you've just got to be stopped.' I was so mad I could have killed him."

Another shadow crossed Jessica's face. "You don't think someone did kill him, do you? The police are asking some very tough questions. Most of us thought murderous thoughts about that creep—but I don't think any of us would ever put them into action."

Walking to work the next morning, Maude tried to think of something pleasant. Even something mundane would do—anything to distract herself from the sights and sounds and feelings of the last evening—and the nightmares that had filled her few hours of sleep.

This morning she found herself obsessed with why Victor had fallen.

Maude wanted to believe Victor had simply done something stupid and slipped from his perch on the window-sill. She knew he'd been sitting there, rehearsing his so-called ad-lib monologue. It was his way. He muttered his way through the stuff—again and again.

But what if he hadn't slipped? What if someone had pushed him to his death? No, that was unthinkable.

Work was the way to clear the mind—but it was going to be difficult to concentrate. Maude's current assignment from the weekend magazine show was one of the silliest stories she'd ever done: an anniversary piece on the National Press Club. Outside of Ottawa, who cared?

Maude had already begun shooting the piece—and, in spite of herself, she'd found it had fascinating elements. She loved the kitchen with all its angst and high drama. Here was a place that took creativity seriously!

When she got to the office, she called the magazine show producer to bring him up to date. "So far, I've got the interview with the chef. He's great. A French chef direct from central casting. We've also shot some of the cover material: you know, the staff peeling and chopping and simmering. I still have an interview to do with the kitchen helper. That's scheduled for late this evening. Apparently he was a sous-chef in China. I've hired a Chinese interpreter because I'll get a better interview if he doesn't have to stumble around in English.

"But the really great pictures will be early this evening: the chef is a fanatic for ceremonies, in the kitchen and in the dining room. Each course is wheeled out to the oohs and aahs of the guests. It's run like a military drill: synchronized watches and all that. Tonight's the Press Club's big anniversary dinner, so it could be quite spectacular."

Maude wound up her conversation and went down to the kitchen to reconfirm everything with the prickly chef.

When she got there, she discovered there was a hitch. Song Ji, the kitchen helper, had been fired. "He is un désastre," the grim-faced chef told her. "He is a clumsy oaf. He shall nevair come into my keetchen again."

"But just yesterday morning you told me he was a treasure," Maude objected. "That's why I shot quite a bit of his work."

"That was yesterday morning."

A day ago, the short, rotund chef had been full of bonhomie, delighted to be the star of a segment on television. Today he was waving his cleaver and grinding his teeth. Maude backed away, but the chef insisted on giving her the details.

"That eediot. He comes back early from his break—and gets in my way. He drops my good knives. Then he implores my forgiveness. I tell him he is an eediot. He steps back. He falls against a cart with a soup tureen. It spills. It takes time to clean it up, to make the silver brilliant again. I have to delay the 'grande entrée' for one complete minute. Can you believe it? One complete minute. It was UN DESASTRE. I told him to leave immédi-atement."

Maude was disappointed. She'd liked the way the little Chinese man went about his work in a serious and purposeful way. "Gee, that's too bad, Chef Lanteigne," she said. "It means I'll have to bring a crew in to shoot footage of someone else. I'm afraid we'll be in your way for another full afternoon."

Chef Lanteigne's face worked through a series of expressions—none of them positive.

"He probably just had a bad night, last night," Maude coaxed. "You did tell me he'd been invaluable in the three months he's been here."

The chef was called away to the phone. In the distance, Maude watched him talk briefly, gesticulating angrily. Rather than hang up, he threw the receiver at the wall. Then he slumped beside it for a moment. He seemed to have exhausted all his emotions. Next, he shrugged wearily, and plodded back to where Maude stood near the service door to the dining room.

"My sous-chef. He has 'la grippe.' His wife says he cannot get out of bed. Tonight of all nights. What can I do? What can I do?"

Maude spread her hands. "There's always Mr. Song," she said.

When she arrived back on the eighth floor, Maude bumped into Amir's sister, Miriam, at the elevator doors. The young woman was fighting back tears.

"Don't tell me something more has happened," Maude asked her.

Young Miriam nodded. "They've taken my brother to the police station for more questioning."

Maude's heart sank as she watched the elevator doors close. Maude liked the young woman—had liked her ever since she'd begun hanging around the bureau, as a journalism student, picking up the odd research job. She must be very worried.

And Amir? Under suspicion? Maude shook her head. Impossible. He was a respected cameraman—not a murderer. She wandered around for a few minutes, trying to get her head around her work. She found she couldn't settle on anything. Eventually she sat down with a pencil and paper and began to draw a time-line that covered a half hour from 7:30 to 8:00 the previous evening. She moved around the office asking questions and filling in the details. Then she went to see her bureau chief.

"O.K., Snoop," Frank said. "What have you got?"

Maude closed the door while he forwarded his phone to the receptionist. "What do you mean—Snoop?" she objected.

"You're a reporter? You're nosy. It's just that your nose is longer than most."

"I have a very nice nose."

"Come on, Maude. Get on with it."

Maude opened her notebook and made herself comfortable. "Well, as you say, I have been nosing around for details—minutes-and-seconds kinds of details. Here's what I've got so far. The planning meeting ended around 7:40. Then it was time to line up the shot for the promo—and run a test with the network. Victor sat on the window-sill and did a run-through while Amir worked. That took four or five minutes, because for once, everything technical was up and running. Are you with me so far?"

Frank nodded. Maude checked her notes again.

"You waited around because you wanted to shout at Victor. You got to it around 7:44 or 7:45. By all accounts the shouting match lasted a couple of minutes. Victor walked out on you, while you were still threatening him with mayhem."

"I did not threaten him."

"Five witnesses say you did. Anyway he went down the corridor, and apparently he gave Miriam's bum a squeeze on the way by, and said, 'How ya' doin' sweetheart?'

"At about 7:48, he walked back to the window, looked Amir in the eye, and shouted out, 'Miriam, baby, come and keep me company until my big moment.'

"Amir was outraged. He walked up to him, nose-to-nose and said: 'You go near my sister again, and you will not live to see darkness fall. You understand?' He stormed off. What he'd do if he found out Victor had already taken Miriam to bed—while big brother was out on the campaign trail—I don't know."

"Are you sure about that?"

"Ninety-five percent sure. It was when Victor came up to Ottawa to prep for the election-night coverage. He was staying at the Hilton. I went over to do an interview with those pollsters. And who walks out of the elevator, holding hands and looking flushed but Victor and Miriam?"

"She's just a kid. She must be twenty years younger than he was."

"Pretty soon you'll tell me he was a cad and a bounder. Anyway, back to the events of last night. So Amir storms back to the technical area—which is where I got him to help me find a clip. Meanwhile Victor is rehearsing his promo—and going over the opening lines of the special."

"How do you know that?"

"Jessica was in the work cubicle beside the window. She heard him. So did the production assistant from Toronto and one of the producers. They were in the next cubicle.

"The next thing they know, Amir comes rushing past their workstations towards the window. And then he starts paging Victor. The producer is astounded. She knows she's just heard Victor rehearsing."

"No wonder the police are treating it as a suspicious death," Frank commented. "And the suspicion sure points at Amir."

Maude wanted to go over some of the Press Club footage with George Cromwell. She found him in the editing booth, finishing up another assignment. "It'll just take a few minutes," he said. "Jessica gets dubs of everything she does—not just video—but an audio dub, too."

"An audio dub?"

George shrugged. "Apparently she plays the cassette over and over again in her car, and at her desk."

"She's a real perfectionist, isn't she?"

"You know last spring, how Victor upstaged her during the election-night broadcast?" George asked.

"Hmmmm. It was pretty blatant."

"Blatant? He went on for seven or eight minutes. Well, the guys in Toronto say she played that tape over and over—looking for ways she could trump him—if he ever tried it again.

"Oh by the way," the editor said as he picked up another video cassette, "what do you want me to do with this tape you guys shot in the driveway last night. It's pretty grisly stuff."

"Put it up," Maude said on impulse. "I'll watch it in fast forward."

She watched as much as she could. Fortunately the tape wasn't long. At the end, the camera panned over the entire driveway. Maude noted some miscellaneous trash: orange garbage bags outside the kitchen delivery door; an empty pack of Player's cigarettes; several sheets of dirty newspaper; a couple of crumpled Budweiser beer cans.

She was just about to hand George the first of her Press Club tapes when the receptionist paged her to pick up the phone. It was Chef Lanteigne. Mr. Song Ji would be at work that evening.

Maude and the crew arrived at 7:15, to give them time to set up lights for the grand entry.

"It will 'appen at 7:55 exactement," the chef said with finality. He was briefing them about the evening timetable. "Always it is the same with the Grande Entree: 7:55 p.m. Not a second earlier. Not a second later."

Across the room, Song Ji caught Maude's eye. He nodded and smiled. Then he put a hand to his heart—and nodded and smiled again. Obviously the chef had told him he was getting a second chance because of the television lady. Good, Maude thought. That'll make the interview a lot easier.

Maude busied herself with her notes while the crew set up their lights in the kitchen and dining room. She was pleased when the crew completed the task with a few minutes to spare.

The chef motioned Song Ji to his side. "Everything is in order here. I 'ave only to put the garnishes on the soup. Theeess I do myself." He sounded as though he were instructing a five-year-old. "It is time for you to smoke the cigarette. But you must be back in five minutes—without fail." The chef turned to Maude, rolling his eyes. "Always it is the same. He has to 'ave his feelthy cigarette. He goes at précisement 7:49."

Song Ji made his way to the kitchen door. Maude nodded to the translator and they followed him down a corridor into the delivery area. Time for a preliminary chat. Just inside the door, Song Ji pulled out a pack of cigarettes and prepared to light up.

"We don't mind going outside with you if you want to smoke," Maude said.

Song Ji shook his head nervously.

"It isn't cold at all tonight." Maude opened the door and looked out. It took her a moment to orient herself. Then she drew in a sharp breath. Victor Todd's body had lain only a few feet away from where she was now standing. Her stomach heaved. She glanced at Song Ji. He looked sick: his mouth was hanging half-open, and his hand shook as he tried to slip his cigarettes back into a pocket. It was a pack of Players'. A dozen connections began to form in Maude's head.

"You saw something out there last night, didn't you? Before the police came. When you went for your cigarette break. Am I right?"

Song Ji composed his face. It was utterly expressionless.

"Is the chef right, Mr. Song? Do you always go for your cigarette at exactly the same time?"

He hesitated. Then he nodded warily.

"What time is that, Mr. Song?"

"I have five minutes after we load the soup tureens," he said through the translator.

"And you must be back one minute before the ceremony. Right?"

He nodded again.

"But last night you didn't smoke your cigarette, did you? You came in earlier than usual—and that's when you got into trouble with the chef."

Reluctantly he agreed she was right.

"And you don't want to go out there tonight, do you?"

She was right about that, too, he said.

"Mr. Song, do you think you could trust me?"

He hesitated again—a very long time—and then he nodded.

"I would like you to come with me to the police. The translator and I will go with you—and we will ensure that you come to no harm. Will you go?"

At that moment, the chef rang a bell. It was six minutes to eight. One minute before the "grande entrée."

For the second night in a row, the night-time network news was to come from Ottawa. Phones were ringing, script assistants were tearing around with copy for editors and reporters. For a moment, in the midst of the hubbub, Maude thought she heard the voices of the Wednesday night political panel. "I thought they pre-taped the panel this afternoon," she said to a passing script assistant.

"They did," he replied.

Maude walked toward the voices. She found they were coming from an audio cassette on Jessica's desk.

"I'm writing my introduction," Jessica told Maude, as she rewound a section. "I just need to review what the panel said about the leadership race."

Maude noticed that Staff Sergeant Jamieson had arrived early for his meeting with Song Ji. "Just a few loose ends to tie up," he said, when Maude offered to help him find an office he could use.

Once she had him installed, she went to her desk to pick up her notes, and then out into the corridor, where she began to pace back and forth, trying to make sense of what she knew.

Song Ji's stint in the kitchen ended at nine-thirty. At nine, Maude went to Staff Sergeant Jamieson's office, and knocked on his door.

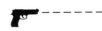

Watching the newscast on the office monitor, Maude decided that Jessica Winchley had the makings of a splendid anchor: she was even more assured than she'd been the night before.

Maude went up to the ninth-floor studio after the newscast.

She watched as Frank enfolded Jessica in a bear hug—and other bureau people crowded round to congratulate her.

Then, when the crowd dissipated, she saw the staff sergeant take Jessica aside. "I'm interested in your tapes and videotapes," Maude heard him say. "I understand you brought some with you from Toronto when you flew in yesterday afternoon. I'm particularly interested in a tape of last spring's election-night broadcast."

Jessica appeared to consider the request for a moment. "I think," she said, "I'd better call my lawyer."

"That's fine, Miss Winchley. I've just obtained a search warrant. I understand you label and initial all your tapes as soon as you get them. We should be able to locate what we need without any difficulty."

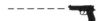

"O.K. O.K. How did you put it all together?"

Frank and Maude were having a late-evening drink in the Press Club bar. They were still absorbing Jessica's arrest. One of their own—well, one of the Toronto bunch—but still, one of their own . . . in handcuffs.

"I don't know whether they'll be able to prove that Jessica did push Victor out that window," Maude said. "But there are some strong indications."

"Like what?"

"Well, a lot of people heard Victor call out to Miriam at about 7:48. Both you and Amir left the area by 7:49. That means that Victor was certainly alone by 7:50. And several people could hear Victor rehearsing his lines in his usual low rehearsal mutter.

"The problem was that Victor was already sprawled on the pavement below—and very dead."

"Huh? Come again?"

"How do I know? Because Mr. Song saw him land at about 7:50. Song Ji, in case you didn't know, is the helper downstairs in the kitchen. When they're preparing dinner, he's allowed exactly five minutes for a cigarette break. His break always begins at exactly 7:49.

"Now, last night, Mr. Song stayed outside for no more than one minute. He returned to the kitchen without taking the time to smoke his cigarette. He was in such a panic that in the space of three or four minutes he left a swath of destruction through the kitchen area.

"I began to make the connection when I saw how upset he was at the thought of going outside for his cigarette break. And then I noticed the pack of cigarettes in his hand. Someone dropped an empty package of the same brand of cigarettes outside in the driveway, near where Victor landed. Hence my first conclusion: Mr. Song saw Victor fall at 7:50, or 7:51 at the latest. Therefore Victor could not have been sitting on that window ledge at 7:55, when Amir arrived to shoot the promo. By then Victor had been dead for five minutes."

Frank frowned. "But that's impossible. You just said several people heard Victor. You can't be in two places at once."

"Exactly. So I began to wonder. Could Mr. Song be wrong about the time? Not bloody likely with a chef who runs his kitchen with the split-second timing of a precision drill.

"So then I asked myself: is it possible that one of the network's star reporters could be wrong about what she heard? What about the young Toronto script assistant? And the others who thought they'd heard Victor, too. What could give all these people the sense Victor was still there?"

Maude took another sip of her drink. "And then I thought about the little tape recorder that Jessica uses to play back broadcast dubs.

"As it turns out, Jessica had a tape of last spring's election broadcast. You remember. That's the one where Victor got to do the seven-minute monologue. I don't think he'd ever done that before. The network brass made it very clear he was never to do it again.

"Now just imagine this. Jessica hears you and Amir make your exit. Remember, she's in the cubicle next to the window area. Let's say she walks in, puts her finger to her lips, and walks over to Victor. Maybe she points to something up on the Hill. He twists around to see what she's talking about. I don't think she planned to kill him. Maybe she only intended to give him a little push. You know, scare him enough to shake him up for the evening. And then maybe that little push feels so good she just keeps pushing . . . until he's gone. Forever."

"I think I'm beginning to see where you're headed," Frank said.

"Jessica is very cool under pressure. So when she thinks to herself, 'Oh my God! What have I done? How can I cover my tracks?' she comes up with a solution. She walks around to her cubicle, pops the election night broadcast into her little cassette player, finds the offending seven minutes of uninterrupted Victor—and eases the level up to about half-volume. That's loud enough for at least two or three other people to hear. It's very close to where Victor had been sitting—and everyone will think that he's doing his usual rehearsal thing. And because it lasts seven minutes or so, it should keep going until someone else comes along. When she hears Amir rushing towards the window, she fades the sound down—and out. The finger of suspicion points at Amir—and she becomes our star news anchor."

"A star for two nights. The shortest star-turn in history." Frank took a puff on his cigar. "So it was just a question of minutes and seconds."

Maude shrugged. "In our business, every minute and second counts."

Wall-to-Wall Crime

Three cops standing there on the spot
Where the late Mr. Smith was shot,
Gently questioned his spouse
Who'd been alone in the house
To see if she had done it or not.

The crime scene they couldn't ignore
For the carpet was covered with gore.
Said Mrs. Smith, "I don't mind,
Though your concern is quite kind,
I was wanting to change the decor."

Joy Hewitt Mann

THE SIGN

by Barbara Fradkin

What is this warm, gooey stuff sliding down my cheek? Blood. Oh boy, I'm in trouble. I'm sinking. Can't move. Can't lift my head. Gotta get to the phone, get help. Where am I? Bed. Phone's beside me. Move, fingers. Reach! Jesus, the pain. Like rockets exploding in my head. Ah, there. Can't see the numbers, must be . . .

"Hello, hello, anybody?" Can't hear, can't tell if— "Somebody help me, I think I've got a fucking hole in my head. I'm dying!" I can't feel the phone. I don't think it's in my hand anymore. Can't feel anything . . .

Something's yanking, poking, shoving my head. What's going on? What's that weird hiss, and this crap in my mouth? Murmurs, floating, lights dancing and weaving . . . Jesus, I can't open my eyes. Can't move. Muscles of mush, brain of cobwebs. Can't think. People are whispering. Grim, fancy words—vertebrae, hemorrhage, brain stem. Can't make out what . . .

Ah, it's quiet now except for the hiss. The thing is still in my mouth; it tastes like rubber. I can't spit it out. Can't move my tongue. Fuck, can't move anything. Help! Somebody! Anybody out there? I can't mo-o-ove!

Ben boy, you're in real trouble. This is way worse than the bar brawls or the times you got piss-drunk and woke up the next afternoon in some strange broad's bed. I don't even know what city I'm in. What the hell happened? I can't remember a fucking thing. Wait, I was in bed asleep— yeah, just a regular bed, regular sleep, I'm sure—and the next thing I can remember is lying on this bed in the hospital. I think I'm lying in bed, but I can't feel myself. I'm a head, that's all.

Fuck!

Easy, Ben boy. No point freaking out. It's just a nightmare, God's idea of justice. The fog will pass and you'll wake up soon.

What's that sound? A door opening. Footsteps, hard and clattering. Another set following, slower, softer. Nurses, maybe? To tell me I'll be all right?

"Can he hear us?"

The doctors think not, honey. His brain is badly swollen and he's probably still in a coma."

Not nurses. Patricia! Beautiful, drive-me-wild, don't-touch-me Patricia. Is this a dream? No, I was at your house in Ottawa when this happened. You called me. Your mother's dying, you said. But why did you really call me after all these years? After all the times I begged and you refused. "Let me help you,' I said, "at least for the boy's sake." "I don't need your kind of help, especially not with Scott." And then after fifteen years of blaming me, you invite me to visit. Why? To do this to me?

"He looks so still. Is he ever going to wake up?"

"It's too early to tell. The doctors say the damage to the brain stem is pretty severe. The ventilator is all that's keeping him alive."

You wish. Is that triumph I hear in your voice, Patricia? No tremor, no regret? Well, you're wrong, girl, there's a lot more life to me than that machine. Don't start spending my money just yet!

"Mom, the cops were at the house again today while you were at work."

"Did Gran talk to them?"

"She was asleep. At least pretending to be. But . . . they found your nightgown."

"What nightgown?"

"The pink one. The one you threw in the garbage."

The pink nightgown. That fucking nun's outfit! You were wearing it the night this happened, and I remember you came to my room. You stood over my bed, shaking your fists at me like old times. Your eyes blazing, your cheeks scarlet. You turned me down, I remember now. After fifteen fucking years, when I'd offered you all my money on a platter, you had the nerve to say no. And you threw the D-word in my face again. You always knew how to push my buttons. Next to Saint David, no one could compare. You'd rather keep on fucking his ghost till you're old and gray, when you could have had a real live man who's better in bed than my limpdick of a brother ever was.

"Why'd you throw it out anyway?"

"Because it was torn."

"Mom, the cops are going to think that's fishy."

"Why should they? What's wrong with throwing out an old nightgown?"

"Because they didn't find any sign of burglars, the windows weren't broken, and the doors were locked. They're going to figure it was one of us three. Now you've thrown out the nightgown you were wearing that night, and Gran is acting all weird."

Is that fear I hear in the smug little punk's voice? Fear of what? What do you know that you're afraid the cops will find out? What happened that night?

"What do you mean—weird?"

"She's hardly talking to us. And why didn't she come with us to visit him?"

"This is a shock for her, honey. Uncle Ben was her son, and remember she's not well."

Oh yes, the old crone. Hah! She'll live to a hundred, clutching her chest and quaking over her cane. She's not visiting me because she hates my guts. Being born after David was my first mistake. Surviving the crash that killed David—that was my second. And making money, without her help and without the farm, was my third. Her and the fucking family farm that's been in the Murphy family for six generations—now owned by some Yank from Buffalo, who had the good sense to let it go to scrub. That's my fault too, of course. If David was alive . . .

"Mom, the cops aren't going to give up. They were searching the whole house for the weapon. And Mom, I can't find that little axe."

"Axe! Scott! Why were you looking for the axe?"

"Well. I . . ." Feet shuffled. "I got to thinking. With all that blood, it had to be something sharp."

"Scott, stay out of it. Perhaps the axe is lost, I haven't seen it in months."

"It was by the back door. You used it to chop up the Christmas tree, remember?"

"That was months ago! Forget the police. All we have to do it stick to our story; we were all in our beds by eleven and we didn't hear a thing."

"What if my friends rat on me? What if the neighbours saw the lights? What if someone heard the argument?"

"What argument?"

"The one you and Uncle Ben had about me in the middle of the night."

The argument! It's coming back to me now. Yes, beautiful Patricia, he's stumped you there. You were probably hoping he'd fallen asleep. He'd sneaked in the side door just before three, hoping we wouldn't hear. High as a fucking kite, crashing into the furniture. The boy needs a man's hand, been mollycoddled by women all his life. That's why you asked me to visit, isn't it? Not because the old crone was dying, but because the boy was going to hell. So why did you fight me when I tried to set him straight? He doesn't need hand holding or talking to, he needs a good swift kick in the ass.

"You . . . heard us?"

"You guys were screaming. He said I used drugs, which is ridiculous. I come in a little late and he throws a hairy. Where does he get off playing Daddy anyway! If I wanted a father, I sure as hell wouldn't pick him! He hasn't shown his face around us since I was born and suddenly he's leaving us all his money, so he figures he can tell me how to live. No more drugs, no more skipping school, no more lying to you. Total Nazi! I told him to get out of my face and I went to bed. That's when I heard you fighting with him."

I remember that, Patricia. You stormed into my bedroom, pistols blazing, gave me twenty-four hours to leave town. Three-thirty in the morning; you threw all the lights on and screeched like a banshee. Scott's right, the neighbours could be a problem.

"What else did you hear?"

"Mom, it's not important. I don't really remember, I was pretty tired."

Try stoned, kid. Beyond reason and control. Saying get out of my face doesn't begin to cover what you did that night. I remember that clear as day. You chucked a lamp at me, took me by the throat and tried to shove me through the wall. Lucky for you I just threw you across the room. I could have snapped your puny back in two.

"Scott, if you heard anything . . . Whatever you think you heard, it wasn't true. Ben's a manipulator and a liar, and you must never believe a word he says. He'd do anything to get what he wants. I had hoped he'd changed, but he hasn't."

"Well, I did hear him say he was going to disinherit us if I didn't smarten up and if you wouldn't . . . you know."

"But I didn't care! You must believe that, honey. The money wasn't worth it. I would never, ever do something like that just for the money."

"We need the money, Mom."

"I support us perfectly well. I know there aren't many frills, but we have a house, meals on the table, clothes on our backs, and we live with honour. That's how your father would have wanted us to live."

"My father. Right. So why didn't he stick around to help? All this honour crap is great, Mom, but he checked out and left you holding the ball."

"He wasn't driving the car, sweetie. Uncle Ben was. Your father would never have been so reckless."

You got that right, princess. Old stick-in-the-mud David didn't even know what fun was! Never took a risk, never broke a rule. The Murphies had been Valley farmers for a hundred and fifty years, so don't even think of rocking the boat. That worthless piece of scrub ran the old man into the ground before he was sixty, but oh no, I was supposed to take it on. Not on your life, Ma.

"Did Dad and Uncle Ben look alike?"

"What makes you ask that?"

"Just wondering what Dad looked like. Don't freak out."

"I'm not. I'm sorry, it's just imagining the two of them in the same gene pool. I suppose they did look alike. Ben's taller and heavier, but they had the same wavy hair and the same Irish blue eyes."

"Like mine."

"Yes, like yours. You know, I think we've been here long enough. He doesn't even know we're here."

"I think he opened his eyes."

"What! Did he?"

Did I? Can I move anything? Yes, my tongue. Hah! I can move my tongue!

"Mom, what if he wakes up!"

"I—I'm sure he won't. The doctors aren't hopeful. It was probably just muscle spasms."

"But he could know. He could be lying there listening. Remembering— "

"He's not! Let's go, Scott. I don't like to leave Gran alone too long."

Boy, you hustled him out of here fast enough. Scared I'd wake up? Scared I'd remember? It's coming. Nothing can keep Ben Murphy down forever. Today my tongue, tomorrow my toes! I'll find out which member of my loving family smashed my head in and left me to die. And then, boy . . . payback time.

God, I wish someone would tell me what time it is. Is it still today? Did I sleep? I think they gave me a shot. How's the old body today? Can I still move my tongue? Yes! Piece of cake. My eyes? Yeah, I can feel them blink today. I can't move my head, though, it feels like it's in a vice. Fingers and toes . . . Not there yet, but I'm making progress. The brain is much sharper. I'll beat them all—the doctors, my mother, Patricia, Scott. All the people who hope I'll die and take the secret of my murder to the grave. Boy, are they in for a shock!

What's that? Someone's in the room. I can hear breathing. The old crone! I'd recognize that death rattle anywhere. Come to visit me, Ma? To cry, or to gloat? You've wished me dead for years; don't think I've forgotten the curse you laid on me fifteen years ago over David's grave.

David. Big brother David.

Gone.

Talk to me, Ma. Don't just sit there rattling. Tell me you're sorry for all the bad things you did to me, for the belt and the closet and the cold, silent nights. Tell me you'll miss me. Beg me not to die. Don't you see this is your last chance to say I love you to your fucking son! I didn't kill David, you know. I've gone around that curve at that speed a hundred times. David was angry at me and giving me the You're-a-worthless-piece-of-shit speech he learnt from you. He made me mad, and distracted me from the wheel for just that second. Hell, do you think I wanted him dead? Sometimes maybe, yeah. I'd picture Patricia and me . . . But I nearly killed myself in that crash. Do you think I intended that? Do you know how many times I've relived that curve, told David to shut up, and kept my eyes on the road? I'd have given up all my dreams of Patricia and our future to have David back running that goddamn farm for you. You should have known that, Ma. Did you really think I was such a monster? I was a wild kid; I lied, I cheated—all right, I stole a couple of cars too—but it was all kidstuff. I didn't kill David and I didn't kill Dad. No matter how black you want to paint me, the fact is, what with losing David and then the farm, Dad just gave up living. You lost him, but I lost him too. You never thought about that. It was always you, poor you, who'd lost everything. Your precious David, your precious Jack, your precious fucking farm. Even my money was too worthless for you. You went to live with precious David's widow instead, to be near fucking precious David's son. But you won't get David back through them.

Now's your chance. I'm not supposed to hear, see, think, or feel, so now's your chance to say something. Tell me what's real, deep down in that heart of yours, if it's there. Underneath the pride and the bitterness and the Murphy rules of right and wrong. Someone tried to kill your son, Ma. I'm lying in a hospital bed tied to tubes and breathing by machine, just like David was. Doesn't it bring back memories, doesn't it grab you somewhere? Make you feel something?

Talk to me, you fucking bitch! I don't ask for much, just one little sign. Mothers should love their sons, the way Patricia loves that puny punk of hers. Even when he's robbing her blind, she loves him. I was like Scott, Ma! Confused, trapped, mad at the world, and thumbing my nose. Patricia wouldn't leave Scott twisting in the wind. I could use some of that. That's all I'm asking. For someone to let me in.

Patricia did, once. You never knew that, did you? No one ever did except Patricia, me, and David on the day he died. He found us in the woodshed. She was wild back then, full of life and passion. She saw stuff in me that no one else ever did. There was a kind of fire between us that was never there with David. She said so herself. She said I was deeper, scarier, and more loving than he was. She saw that in me once, Ma. Before guilt and duty killed it, and she decided to live her life in his memory. Raise my son in his memory. David. Always goddamn David!

Wow! What was that? Something's on my arm. I can feel my arm! You're touching it, Ma. You're squeezing it. Is that the sign? You're leaning closer, I can hear your breath rattling in my ear. Do you want to say something to me, Ma?

Boy, your grip is strong. For an old lady who weighs ninety pounds if you're lucky, you still pack some muscle. Must be all those years on the farm, hauling feed and chopping wood. Even after Dad died, trying to keep that little bit of it running by yourself till the old ticker called it quits. I bet you could still split a cord of wood, heave the axe over your head, and—

Jesus.

The axe. I remember seeing the axe, Ma. Just a flash out of the corner of my eye. Please tell me it isn't true.

It could have been Scott, still coked up; he was right across the hall too. Or Patricia. We were screaming like lunatics. I got carried away and so did she. Too many secrets buried too long. I was sick of being on the outside. I wanted in. Was that too much to ask? My son was fifteen years old—when would she let me call him mine? I know I shouldn't have grabbed her. I shouldn't have threatened to tell him. I should have been patient and understanding, then maybe she'd have told him herself. But we got wild that night, and you know how all the bad stuff in me comes out when I get mad. Whatever I said, if you heard it, about David and Dad and the farm and Scott—I didn't mean half of it. Talk to me, Ma. Tell me you know that.

"You never could do anything right for me, could you, boy. You and that thick skull of yours. You wouldn't even die like I wanted you to."

THE LITTLE TREASURES

by Audrey Jessup

I met Selena shortly after I moved into the apartment building on Somerset Street. She was struggling to balance a bag of groceries while she inserted her key in the lock with her arthritic hands, and her long leopard-print chiffon scarf had slipped to the ground and tangled around her feet. Our lout of a janitor just stood there, watching her distress. I slung my purse over my shoulder and went to help, offering to carry her load up to her apartment. It turned out we both lived on the fifth floor, at opposite ends of the hall.

"It is nice to have somebody young as a neighbour," she said, and invited me in for a cup of lemon tea. I didn't want to get involved and I was going to decline, but there was something in her black-rimmed eyes that spoke to me of loneliness, and I knew something about that, so I accepted. I wondered afterwards if her trusting friendliness, and the loneliness, had been what led to her death.

"You are so kind," she said in her deep, gravelly voice, as I deposited the groceries on the kitchen counter. "Now we will take tea."

She used a plastic jug to fill the kettle, and when she had finished, the water tap was still dripping. I reached over to turn it off but she called to me sharply, "No, don't do that." I must have looked surprised because she laughed apologetically. "I'm sorry," she said, "but if you close the tap, I will not be able to open it again. I have to have everything loose, you see." She held up her twisted hands and shrugged. "You get used to the drip, drip, drip," she said. "But perhaps you will carry the tray into the salon." The tray held two glasses in filigree silver holders, long silver spoons, lemon slices, and sugar. She added a tall silver pot with a domed lid crowned with a rampant silver bear. I picked up the tray and followed her.

I stepped into the "salon" and came to a dead stop. My Presbyterian genes all snapped up their heads. I had walked through a magic curtain into the Arabian Nights. The walls were draped with fringed silk shawls in soft patterns of rose and old gold. Two divans, forming an L, were covered in throws striped in red, gold, and blue and piled with a multitude of cushions of all shapes, sizes, and colours. Oriental rugs in rich reds and blues overlapped one another, and a set of four black tables, inlaid with mother of pearl and cornered in studded brass, were placed before the couches. The dark-red velvet drapes were drawn back, but the pink sheer curtains filtered the daylight into a rosy glow. Floor lamps in the shape of upturned lotus blossoms were placed here and there. It was like a stage set for some eastern extravaganza, and I discovered later that's exactly what it was.

Selena chuckled at my expression. "It is a little surprise, no?" She motioned me to sit beside her on a divan.

Selena herself was as exotic as her surroundings. She must have been about sixty-five, but her hair was jet black and I suspected she dyed it herself because the tops of her ears were black, too. She wore heavy make-up, using kohl around her eyes with a rather unsteady hand. She was wearing a long skirt and loose top of fine pleated lawn printed in shades of rust and cream, and round her tiny waist she wore an elaborate silver link belt. Her earrings almost touched her shoulders and tinkled when she moved her head.

As she poured the tea, I had a chance to look around the room more closely. The only exception to the eastern theme was a glass-fronted cupboard in the corner which seemed to contain knick-knacks.

"Ah, you have noticed my little treasures," she said, her throaty voice rolling the first syllable of "treasures." "They are my memories—and perhaps my future!"

She had been, I learned, a ballet dancer, and besides the "memories" in the cupboard she had plenty of reminders of her former life. Those rich salon furnishings had come from a production of *Scheherezade*, and the hallway of her apartment was covered with photographs of her in her heyday.

"We will bring them into the salon," she said. "The light is broken out there, and the janitor does not come to fix."

We sat on the divan and looked at pictures of Selena as Odile in *Swan Lake*, Selena as Giselle; as Sleeping Beauty; as Salome; and, most of all, as Scheherezade.

"It was my triumph," she exclaimed. "The critics said never before had there been such a Scheherezade. Paris and London went mad over me." She held the picture clutched to her chest, her eyes half-closed, as she re-lived the moment, swaying slightly to imagined music. I could almost hear the applause.

I was leery of friendships, knowing how easily they could end in betrayal, but somehow I gradually fell into the habit of helping Selena with her shopping on Saturday morning and dropping in sometimes during the week when I got home from work. I had avoided getting involved with people on a personal level since I came to Ottawa, and I enjoyed hearing Selena's stories of backstage intrigue. It was a far cry from my upbringing on the prairies and my job as a bank economist.

She always wore the same kind of loose, flowing garments, partly because they were easier for her to put on but also, I suspected, in an effort to preserve the illusion of grace which had been so eroded by the arthritis in her hands and feet. I knew some of the other tenants laughed at her, but I admired her gallant struggle not to lose her identity. I even got used to the dripping taps and lids that fell off jars when you picked them up.

"Why do you not find a young man?" asked Selena one day. "A career is not enough. You cannot wrap your arms around a bank statement."

I didn't want to explain I'd already had a young man, thank you, and it hadn't worked out. I fenced by saying, "But you had a wonderful career, Selena."

She looked at me with those black-rimmed eyes and shook her head. "Yes, then. But what about now? All I have are my little treasures. They do not keep me warm at night."

Her "treasures" had all been gifts from admirers and were quite an eclectic mixture. There was Lalique crystal (Ah, Louis, he was so handsome); lovely old silver, intricately worked, (Franz, an Austrian nobleman— very demanding); enamelled boxes, one with a crest (Don't let anyone tell you the English are cold, chérie); and several pieces of jewellery which she kept in boxes in the drawers in the lower part of the cupboard. The pièce de résistance, though, given pride of place right in the centre of the centre shelf, was her Fabergé egg (Ah, Igor, Igor, my Russian prince, so Slavic, so passionate).

"Is it really a Fabergé egg?" I asked.

Selena narrowed her eyes and smiled. "What do you think?"

I shook my head. "It's certainly lovely," I said, "but I didn't think there were any left outside the big collections."

Selena seemed to consider for a moment. "Well, I will tell you," she said. "This one was made for a rather naughty joke, so the family always kept it quiet. Come tomorrow and bring your plastic apron and I will show you."

When I arrived the next day with my apron, she fished in the front of her blouse, brought out a key on a chain and unlocked the cabinet.

Selena carefully lifted the egg off its stand and handed it to me. It was made of porcelain and decorated with a floral design which was embellished with jewels, sapphires, emeralds, opals, and pearls, and at the very top, a small crown with a large diamond. If all those jewels were genuine, it was worth a king's ransom.

"Why don't you open it?" said Selena. "Just press that gold button on the back."

Rather warily I did so and SPLAT!—a jet of bright yellow squirted down the front of the apron.

Selena laughed heartily, especially when I saw the tiny figure of a naked man inside the open egg. It was a Russian version of the Mannikin Pis.

She handed me paper towels to wipe off the apron. "It's food colouring," she said, "but it stains, you know. Fortunately I was not wearing a chemise when Igor gave it to me, but I had to soak in the tub for hours to get the marks off." She smiled wickedly. "That is not so bad, though, when you have company, and a bottle of champagne." She sighed. "Ah, we had such good times."

She had some of the yellow mixture left, and she showed me how to refill the little reservoir in the egg. "It was Igor's father who had it made," she told me, "but he died in the Revolution before he had a chance to give it to his petite amie."

Selena told me she had been born near Leningrad and her career had taken her all over Europe, but she never explained how she had ended up living on Somerset Street in Ottawa. The only thing I felt pretty certain of was that a man had been involved. Had a diplomat brought her here and then had to go home, leaving her behind? She never mentioned it, and I didn't like to pry.

I knew from various remarks she had made that not all her "friendships" had been happy. Gustav had broken her nose in a jealous temper, and Franco had chased her down a street in Monte Carlo brandishing a horsewhip.

"But he chased me right into the arms of Gérard," she chuckled. "When you are part of life, you have some good and some not-so-good times." She shrugged. "And now and again, it is the bad things that lead to the good ones. But you have to be there, chérie, you have to be part of it. Am I not right?" She cocked her head and looked at me slyly.

I wasn't in any position to comment on Selena's lifestyle, but I did try to point out the foolhardiness of keeping her valuable souvenirs so openly displayed. She merely shrugged.

"I do not want to lock my memories in a bank vault," she said. "They are all I have."

I also suggested perhaps she should not talk about them so freely. Her "little treasures" represented quite a hefty investment, and I knew she didn't have any insurance on them.

I could only hope other people felt the same way as the man who lived next door to Selena. He stopped me in the hall one day after I had just left her apartment.

"Did she invite you in to see her treasures?" he said, with a sly grin.

"Yes, she did," I said cautiously. "Have you seen them?"

He snorted. "Not likely. She asked me, but I wasn't going to get involved. You have to admit she's a bit strange. I figured if her outfits are anything to go by, the treasures are probably chintzy souvenirs of Morocco. Straight out of the bazaar. Am I right?"

I nodded. "You're close," I said, squelching my feeling of disloyalty to Selena.

"I knew it," he whooped. "She looks as if she used to tell fortunes for a living. She's weird, I tell you."

"She used to be a ballerina," I said rather frostily. "A very famous one."

"Is that her story?" he guffawed. "So what's she doing living in this backwater? She's conning you, lady." He was still chuckling as he closed his door.

I didn't really mind his broadcasting his opinion on Selena's treasures. It would protect her from theft. But I did object to his laughing at her and calling her weird. I saw him later in the day talking to our useless lump of a janitor, and he was obviously telling him what I had said.

"Can you imagine that hag up on her toes in a tutu?" he spluttered.

"Next they'll be telling us she was a go-go dancer," the janitor replied, wiggling his hips and stretching his arms upwards until his T-shirt exposed his fat beer belly.

I marched over to them. "I hope when you're her age, you don't have to live with someone as uncaring as you are," I said to Selena's neighbour. "And as for you," I turned to the janitor, "if I hear you making fun of any of the tenants like that again, I'll report you to the owners. And if you don't get her hall light fixed, I'll report that, too."

It made me feel better to stick up for my friend, but I didn't think it would have much effect. I heard them laughing again as I got in the elevator. At least they'd have me to laugh at as well now.

It was about a week after this that Selena excitedly waved a letter in my face.

"I am having a visit. Igor's great-nephew is coming to see me. I wonder if he will look like Igor. He is a Count, you know." Selena was practically jumping up and down with pleasure. "Is he coming from Russia?" I asked.

"No, no. He lives in New York."

"But you've never met him?" I wondered why he had suddenly decided to visit her now. "How did he get your address?"

Selena shrugged. "One Russian tells another Russian, you know. We will take tea." In other words, none of my business.

Selena invited me to join them the day Sergei arrived. Not only did she have lemon tea, she had been to the Rideau Bakery and bought crisp almond cookies and flaky poppy-seed strudel, which, she told me, is very popular in Russia.

Sergei was as handsome as even Selena could have wished. He was about thirty, with very dark hair worn below his ears, sparkling blue eyes and a brilliant smile. His suit looked like Armani. When Selena introduced us, he bowed and kissed my hand. In spite of myself, I knew I was preening.

His manners were as charming as his looks. He flirted slightly with me, a delicate acknowledgment that we were about the same age even if I was Selena's friend, and he was attentive and deferential to Selena. She was entranced, and I could see her blossoming at the attention from this dashing young male.

He was an investment banker in New York, he told us.

Selena clapped her hands. "Oh, la, la. What a coincidence. Two young people with careers in banks."

"What bank are you with, Sergei?" I asked.

He hesitated for a fraction of a second. "I don't think you will know it. It's called the Kalinskaya International Bank. Our clients are mostly ex-patriates from Russia and the other countries which used to be part of the Soviet Union." He smiled disarmingly. "There are a lot of us in the States, you know, and we like to help one another."

It sounded reasonable. I knew many Russians had left that country with fortunes in jewels.

"You will be able to show Sergei around Ottawa," Selena said, turning to me. "You will have lots to talk about. Money is always fascinating."

Sergei and I both burst out laughing.

"I'd be pleased to," I said, "but unfortunately the bank is sending me to a conference in Vancouver tomorrow for a few days, and I thought I would call on my family in Calgary on the way back. How long do you plan on being here, Sergei?"

He shrugged. "I had not quite decided. But now, perhaps, I shall wait for your return."

He gave me a dazzling, intimate smile, and the warning bells went off in my head. I thought it might be as well I was leaving town. I wasn't planning to get involved again, especially with a smooth customer like this one.

In the end I did not stop off in Calgary. I came straight back to Ottawa. The conference in Vancouver was attended by bankers from all over North America, and during a moment of idle chatter with a New York colleague I had mentioned the Kalinskaya Bank. He had never heard of it, and my cautious Scottish heritage made me concerned about Selena. She was so ready to trust people. I didn't want to telephone and frighten her, but I caught the earliest plane home I could. As soon as I had dropped my bag in my apartment, I went down the hall to see her.

She threw her arms around me. "I am so glad you are back. I have missed you. We will take tea, yes?"

As we went into the salon, I noticed the items in the corner cupboard had been rearranged, but I couldn't quite pin down what had changed. Selena's usual insouciance seemed to have deserted her. Her eye make-up was more smudged than usual, and she kept picking up her glass of tea and putting it down without drinking.

"Is Sergei still here?" I asked.

"Oh, yes, yes, he's still here. Somewhere." She picked up her glass and raised it to her lips, then put it down so sharply the tray rattled. "Oh, dear, I do not know what to do." She looked at me with tears in her eyes. "Sergei wants the egg. He says it belongs to his family, and Igor never meant me to keep it."

I gritted my teeth to avoid exploding. I knew that hand-kissing Count was too good to be true. He'd come to Ottawa to bilk Selena of her treasures.

"When did he tell you this?"

"Just yesterday. Until then we had been having such a nice time. He would come every day and bring me little things—chocolates, cookies, a flower—and he would make the lemon tea for us and serve it." She tried to smile. "He even learned to leave the tap dripping."

"But then yesterday he asked you for the egg."

She nodded and a tear slid down her cheek.

"What did you mean, he's here 'somewhere?'" I asked.

Selena dabbed at her eyes with a tiny scrap of lace handkerchief. "I tried to phone him one day. I thought he had said he was at the Chateau, but he was not registered. So I tried the Westin, and then the Sheraton, and then all the hotels I could find, but nobody knew him. I even called the Embassy, but they knew nothing. Of course when he came, I asked him. He was embarrassed. He even cried. He was so ashamed because he couldn't stay in a hotel. He didn't have enough money. He was staying in a room somewhere. He wouldn't even tell me, he said it was so poor." She looked at me with tragic eyes. "Imagine how I felt. My Igor's nephew, staying in a shabby room."

I frowned. "But he was wearing an Armani suit when he arrived. That must have set him back a bundle."

Selena just looked at me and shrugged. "Sometimes one has things, but one does not have cash."

"So you gave him money," I said. I hadn't listened to all her stories about dancers helping one another out in hard times without learning Selena was as soft-hearted a touch as anyone could find.

"Well . . . just a little."

I got up and went over to the corner cupboard. "What happened to the enamel snuffbox with the crest?" I said.

Selena pulled the lace handkerchief backwards and forwards through her twisted fingers. "I gave it to Sergei so he could pawn it," she said in a low voice. "I did not have cash myself."

I was relieved. I thought if she had sold it in a hurry, she probably would have got much less then it was worth. "But you have the pawn ticket?" I said.

"Oh, yes. He brought it to me right away with the money."

"How much did he get?"

Selena's face looked pinched. "Only fifty dollars. I thought my treasures would keep me in my old age. But if that's all they're worth . . . " Her voice trailed off.

I would have bet a dollar to a piece of New York cheesecake Sergei had received more than fifty dollars, but all I said to Selena was: "Of course they're worth more than that, Selena. Pawnbrokers only give a token amount. If you were ever going to sell them, you'd give them to somebody like Christie's, or take them to an antique dealer." She looked slightly less depressed. "So Sergei took the fifty dollars," I said.

"Yes. He was . . . disappointed, of course. He said he wouldn't be able to move anywhere better with such a pittance."

I took her hand in mine. "Selena," I said, as gently as I could, "how do you know Sergei really is who he says he is? I can't find any record of the bank he's supposed to work for."

Selena looked at me wide-eyed. "But who else could he be?" she asked.

"He could be someone who'd heard about your friendship with Prince Igor and knew you had the Fabergé egg. As you said, Russians talk to one another. He could just be trying to take advantage of you."

The tears rolled down her face in black streaks. "But he said they will stop my allowance if I don't give it to him."

"Who will stop what allowance? What does he mean?"

Selena's head drooped. "Igor's family sends me money every month to stay here."

I sat silent, trying to figure this one out.

"You see," Selena said, "Igor died in my apartment in Paris, and it would have been une scandale énorme. So they paid a lot of money to the authorities to hush it up, and they arranged for me to come here."

"How long ago was this?"

"Ten years."

"Well, Selena," I said, "if you've had the egg all that time, I can't see why the family would ask for it now. And above all, I can't see them sending a young guy like Sergei to get it." She looked at me doubtfully. "Think about it for a minute. Wouldn't you expect to get a letter first, and then a call from a family representative, perhaps even a lawyer?"

Selena blinked and wiped her eyes with her wisp of a handkerchief. She looked surprised when it showed black. "I suppose you may be right," she said reluctantly. "But Sergei is a Russian, I'm sure."

"I don't doubt it. But I do doubt he was sent by Igor's family." I tried to figure out what we could do. "Is he supposed to come again today?" I asked.

Selena looked frightened. "Yes. About seven o'clock."

I thought for a moment. It was almost six now. "I think the best thing will be for you to pretend you're out. Don't answer the door," I said. "Or the telephone. No matter how much he knocks, and how often the phone rings. We'll put a note on the door saying you've gone to the theatre and you'll see him tomorrow." I helped her prepare the note. She wrote it in Russian, on scented lilac paper.

"I will take a sleeping potion," she said. "I did not sleep well last night."

"If you give me the pawn ticket, at least I can check on that. I'll come by in the morning before I go to the office. I'll knock three times, like this, so you'll know it's me."

When I left I heard her double lock the door.

I went right over to the pawnshop and presented the ticket. I was pretty sure Sergei had received more than fifty dollars, and I was right. After I forked over one hundred dollars, the clerk opened a brown envelope and out slid . . . Sergei's watch. He hadn't pawned Selena's enamelled box at all, damn him. He was probably holding onto it, knowing he'd get a better price in New York. I took the watch, anyway, because I was too embarrassed to refuse it, and because I thought it might be proof of something or other. That no-good con artist wasn't going to get away with it if I could help it.

As I rounded the corner by the apartment building, still steaming, I saw Sergei in the driveway talking to the janitor. He had Selena's note in his hand and seemed to be explaining what it said. I slipped out of sight and watched. I couldn't hear what they said, but Sergei gestured at the bunch of keys the janitor had on his belt, and I figured he was suggesting they could go into Selena's apartment. I was relieved when he finally walked away. Without even thinking about it, I followed him. At least I could try to find out where he was staying.

I didn't have to go very far. He went into a hotel a couple of streets over. I watched him pick up a key from the desk. So what did this mean? If Selena had tried all the hotels, she must have telephoned this one. Obviously he was not registered under the name he'd given to Selena. Somehow I was not surprised, and I felt doubly pleased I had cut my trip short. I would make sure Selena had nothing more to do with this shyster. The worst that could happen was she would lose one snuffbox.

Selena didn't answer her door the next morning at eight-thirty when I gave our secret knock. I kept trying for fifteen minutes, in case she was having a bath, but when she still didn't answer, I felt something was wrong and called the janitor. He grumbled, but eventually he came lumbering up with keys and we went in.

Selena lay on her back on the floor in the salon, her right cheek pressed into the carpet. Blood had trickled out of her left ear, leaving a caked line down her cheek. The back of her head was caked with blood, too. Her eyes gazed off into nothingness. One of the brass-edged tables had a dark stain on the corner. I felt my stomach heave and I fought down the nausea.

"Jesus," said the janitor.

I made myself go over to her and lean down to check for a pulse. Her skin was cold and waxy-feeling.

"You'd better call the police," I said. He started to move towards the telephone and I caught his arm. "No, you'd better call from your apartment," I said. "We shouldn't touch anything in this room."

He gave me a look which plainly expressed his opinion of women as hysterical creatures, but he left anyway. I went to sit in the kitchen till somebody came. I didn't want to look at that poor little body any more.

On the kitchen counter was the little flowered tray with two glasses in filigree silver holders, two long spoons and cubes of sugar in a crystal bowl. I ran my finger over the filigree holders, remembering all the times I had taken lemon tea with my gallant little friend. I remembered her enthusiasm for life and living, even if it brought disappointments and heartbreak, and I thought of my own life. She may not have had somebody to keep her warm at night, but she did have wonderful and exciting memories—memories she had shared with me. I felt my nose prickle as tears started to form, and I jumped up. I wasn't going to pull back from experience any more, and I was going to start by keeping vigil over my friend's body so she wouldn't lie there alone in her exotic room.

As soon as I returned to the salon I saw it. The door of the corner cupboard was hanging open and the egg, as well as the rest of the enamelled boxes, had gone. Sergei must have come back, thinking the apartment was empty. Selena had surprised him and he had killed her. I shook with rage, and if he'd walked in that minute, I think I'd have strangled him.

When the police arrived, I rushed to tell them about the cupboard and Sergei.

"She kept the key on a chain around her neck," I said, "but he didn't know that."

One of the officers went over and used a pencil to fish out the chain. The key was still there.

The other policeman took me by the arm. "If you'll come into the kitchen, Miss, and sit down, I'd like a description of this Sergei and anything else you can tell us about him. Just how were you involved with the deceased?"

I blinked. He was right. I *was* involved. Despite myself, I had become involved in a friendship again. And it had been good.

I told him what Sergei looked like, and where he was staying. "He's not registered under the name he gave Selena," I said, "but how many good-looking Russians can there be staying at the hotel?"

The officer only nodded but when he telephoned the station to report, he suggested that someone be sent to have Sergei picked up. "We just want to talk to him," he said.

"He was after her treasures," I said indignantly. "He'd already stolen a valuable snuffbox." I gave him Sergei's watch and told him how he had bilked Selena. "He probably thought she wouldn't redeem the pawn ticket until after he'd left town. He tried to soften her up into giving him the egg," I said. "He'd bring her chocolates and make her lemon tea. He must have been getting impatient and seized the chance when he thought she was out for the evening." I knew I would always feel guilty for having persuaded Selena to put that note on the door.

"Do you have any proof your friend didn't just give him the snuffbox?" the officer said. His tone was kind, and I knew he was trying to tell me as gently as possible that it would be hopeless trying to nail Sergei for the theft.

I stared at the silver tray with the glasses in filigree holders, railing inwardly against the stupidity of the law. Surely, though, Sergei couldn't have come into the apartment last night and not left some evidence. I looked around, and suddenly I realized something was missing.

"But it couldn't have been Sergei," I babbled. "The tap isn't dripping."

The policeman wasn't at all convinced by my explanation, I could tell, but he didn't argue.

"Let's get the janitor up here, Tom," he said to his partner. "He may have seen someone coming in or out last night."

While he waited, he went to look at the pictures in the hall. "She seems to have been quite a star," he said.

"Yes. If you bring them into the kitchen, you'll see . . . " My voice trailed off. He could see them perfectly clearly in the hall.

The light had been fixed.

"I know who did it," I cried. "I know who stole the egg. It wasn't Sergei, Officer. He wasn't the only one who thought the apartment would be empty last night." As quickly and as plainly as I could, I told him about the egg and the yellow food colouring.

The janitor tried to claim those were nicotine stains on his fingers.

THE WHITE SWAN CAPER

by Linda Wiken

It's not that I don't like swans. I do. Sort of.

Swan Lake was the first and only ballet I cried through. I have my Mom's collection of glass swans on display—my sister got the Royal Doulton figurines. And I've even been known to feed the swans that cluster near Billings Bridge in the Rideau River.

It's just, I didn't get even mildly upset when reading the brief two-paragraph report on the second page of the Citylife section of the *Ottawa Citizen*. All it said was the white swans were gone. Or in hiding. They'd done that one year previously, sort of disappeared round about the time the city was due to gather them up for winter storage. The interesting thing this time was that the black swans remained.

I wouldn't have drawn the case either, except that my old school chum, Alan Dawson, asked the staff sergeant to assign me. And, being low person on the detective totem pole, I got it. The police always like to be seen as co-operating with city hall.

"Listen, Julie. I'm really glad you've been put in charge of the case," Alan assured me when I called to get more details from him. "I trust you. I know you'll take it seriously and follow through. This is real swell of you."

Alan talks like that. Glad, swell, a lot of "neats" also. Like he's caught in a time warp of our high-school years even though they ended a decade ago. I tried to steer him away from the accolades onto the meat of the matter.

Since Alan is in charge of the care and feeding of all the swans, he sounded quite upset when he focused on their collective disappearance. Alan talks about them as if they were his children so he was certain they'd been kidnapped and a ransom note would soon follow.

Which would mean we were dealing with a really dumb perpetrator here. Everyone knows the black swans are the valuable ones, so if anyone were thinking of a heist and fencing them, they should have gone for the black.

I tried to make a list of motives. Serious ones. But my eyes kept wandering to Detective Brian Noble who hovers at the desk adjacent to mine. He'd drawn a break-and-enter, number 1800-plus in our district this year, but this one interested me. An artsy burglar had made off with a valuable Andrew Wyeth painting and a selection of uncut gems.

Damn Alan Dawson and Miss Montgomery's English Lit class. If I hadn't taken pity on his term paper, I'd be immersed in Wyeth right now.

Not really.

Junior detectives do not get the high-profile cases. I'd already learned that. What I hadn't yet found out was how long one remains in the junior classification. Especially if that junior is a female.

I did know that most of the old boys thought I'd make first grade damn quick, now that the city had a female inspector in Criminal Investigations. But she'd set me straight on that within a few days of getting settled behind her baffle. She knew the talk and told me I'd have to work harder to prove them all wrong. Not that I hadn't planned on earning my rank but I hadn't counted on double jeopardy.

Brian drew me back to my present predicament, asking, "Any luck?"

He smirked.

I allowed him that, since he'd taken the trouble over the past few months to show me the ropes, on the QT.

"Not so's you'd notice. It beats me why anyone would want to make off with the white swans."

I heard a desk drawer roll shut to my left. "Maybe they're doing new ads for paper towels."

I ignored the remark made by Detective Sergeant John "The Jerk" Myers. I didn't feel comfortable enough in the job to joke with him.

"When in doubt . . .," Brian left it wide open.

"Check out the scene of the crime," I finished for him. Standard fare for us both.

My purse got stuck on the latch of the drawer I'd stuffed it into. A button on my new leather jacket needed coaxing to dislodge from a crack in the arm of the chair. And I felt a run in my pantyhose broaden in scope and appearance as I stood up. Not an auspicious way to begin an investigation.

Fortunately, I drew car number 4286, one of the new unmarked Caprices, which meant the heater should be working. The weather channel had shown a windchill this morning, even though there was a week left in September.

Maybe someone had taken pity on the swans and given them a nice warm place to stay. And that someone would call Alan Dawson and tell him where to find his feathered friends. Which would free me to assist Brian Noble.

And maybe, Santa would bring me a nice promotion.

I cursed my short jacket, short skirt, and new flats as I tramped across the lawn from the parking lot to the river's edge. If I hadn't been asked out to lunch, I'd be wearing sneakers and jeans.

The Rideau River looked the same as usual—scummy with odds and ends of sticks and stumps protruding everywhere. Some ducks. No swans, though.

The spot was ideal for a swan-napping, no doubt about it. A four-lane stretch carried motorists past at a fair clip, ensuring drivers wouldn't be watching the scenery. On the other side of the roadway was the Billings Bridge Mall, several playing fields, and way back, the R.A. recreation centre. It was all guaranteed to offer privacy to anyone who wanted to meditate by the water. Or do other things.

The swans had last been spotted here by a city crew doing a general park clean-up Tuesday afternoon. Later that day, a concerned citizen called from a payphone at the mall and said a man was trying to grab a swan.

We're into DPR's these days. That's "Delayed Police Response," a method by which fewer officers handle more calls. "Male snatching swan" didn't rate a priority. By the time a patrol car pulled into the lot several hours later, it was empty.

A report was filed with the city, though, and by the end of the day, Alan Dawson had made the rounds of the swans' favourite dives and come up empty. Except for the four black ones. The next morning—today—the report landed on my desk. The trail had grown cold.

I hiked back to the car and located some binoculars in the trunk. The other side of the river had houses bordering it. Maybe someone, a little old person with nothing better to do, spent each day watching the waters flow. I knew there was at least one nursing home somewhere across the way. I perched on a log and slowly scanned the back windows. Nothing.

Of course, the crime had taken place in the late afternoon. I'd return with my binocs, and suitable shoes, at the appropriate hour.

It took about five seconds for me to realize what I was staring at. And one second for "it" to disappear. Someone had been watching me watching across the river. I slowly took in the design of the house, its colour, and then counted to the end of the street. This person might be shy but he/she was the closest to a lead I had.

Getting to the house was not as easy as I'd thought. After several wrong turns on dead-end streets, I finally pulled up in front of the two-storey, white clapboard house. It looked vintage for the area, probably forty-five years old. The owner obviously had a green thumb.

The doorbell was answered by a woman a few years younger than me, probably in her late twenties. She looked curious and harried, so I skipped the pleasantries.

"I'm Detective Kellog with the Ottawa Police. I'm investigating the disappearance of the city's swans from the Rideau River. I'd like to ask you a few questions."

I wasn't sure if her hesitation meant she was busy or dumbfounded. I hadn't realized how silly the whole thing sounded until I said it out loud.

A yelp from somewhere in the house startled us both.

"My son," she said with an apologetic smile. "Please, come in."

I waited in the small hallway while she hurried to the back. After a few minutes of obstinate child sounds, she came back.

"I don't know how I can help, Detective, but you can ask away. Could we talk in the kitchen though? My son's out there. I'm Jessie Shasta, by the way."

I followed her to a large, bright kitchen that ran the width of the house. At one end, a boy about four sat with his leg propped up on a foot stool. A colourful cast ran from mid-thigh to his toes. His mom introduced him as Sammy and explained he was recovering from a compound fracture.

Sammy smiled at my greeting but it faded fast when his Mom explained I was a cop.

My shy spy?

"Mrs. Shasta, do you mind if I ask Sammy a few questions?"

She looked startled but agreed.

I squatted beside his chair, giving him the height advantage.

"Sammy, do you like playing 'I spy?'"

He nodded. Still hesitant.

"I was just over there," I pointed to the good view of the other side of the river, "and I spied with my binoculars someone looking my way. Was it you?"

He looked at his Mom, his panic obvious.

"It's all right," I added hastily. "You're not in any kind of trouble. In fact, I'm hoping you were playing 'I spy' earlier this week. Because I really need your help, if you were."

He took a few seconds to digest this and looked at his Mom again. She nodded.

"I spied you," he said proudly and held up a small but powerful pair of binoculars.

"Good. Good. Now, have you ever spied the white swans swimming along the river?"

He nodded. "Swans."

"Did you see them two days ago?" My turn to look at his Mom. How do kids distinguish days past?

"You remember," she said helpfully, "the day Uncle Mike came for supper." Sammy nodded. "You were watching with your spy glasses while I made supper."

"Uh-huh."

"Did you see someone playing with the swans?" I asked.

"Uh-huh."

Great. Now we were getting somewhere. "Was it a man or a woman?"

"A man."

"And what did he do?"

"He gave the swans supper."

"Did you see him feeding the swans?"

"He put them in his truck."

"So, why do you think he was feeding them?"

"Because he was the carrot man."

Carrot man. Did he have red hair? Did he carry a Fresh Fruit bag? I looked at his Mom for guidance but she seemed to think we were doing okay on our own.

"Did he put the swans back in the water after he'd fed them?"

"Nope. He drove them away."

My swan-napper, at last. "Was there writing on the truck? Could you read a name?"

His Mom shook her head just as I realized the dumb mistake. "Did the truck have letters on it?" I quickly revised.

"Yup. And carrots."

Ah-hah. A vegetable delivery truck? His Mom had reached the same conclusion.

"That's not our vegetable man," she assured me. "His truck has lettuce and tomatoes on the side."

"There's only one in this area?" I stood and stretched my cramped legs.

"Yes. It's like the chip wagons, they each have their own territory. I haven't a clue who drives a carrot truck."

"Maybe your man knows. Could I have his name and phone number, please?"

"His name, yes. But that's all I know, except that he's from Leitrim."

I took down his name, then thanked Sammy for his help. I also made a note, when back in my car, to arrange for him to be taken on a ride by one of the patrol officers. Lights, sirens, the works. Kids love that. Big kids, too.

That's why I'm a cop.

Mrs. Shasta's vegetable man told me to try the Broughton brothers in Kemptville. I did, the next morning, but didn't get an answer by phone, so thought it was time for a drive out to the country. The good sergeant didn't object when I pointed out that I hadn't seen said suspicious vehicle the day before and would be wasting a lot of time and gas driving around looking for it. Time/budget management was a high priority for the Ottawa Police Services this year. Even more to the point, I think the prospect of having me out of the office for the entire afternoon appealed to him.

Brian Noble winked and warned me to beware of overpriced rutabagas.

It takes forty minutes to reach the bustling village of Kemptville. That gave me time to enjoy the scenery and come up with a plan since I doubted my swan-nappers were just waiting to confess.

I checked in at the local cop shop, partly because of protocol, partly for directions to the farm, but mainly to see if I could re-kindle any sparks with a certain Ontario Provincial Police constable.

I lucked in to the first part—Constable Silver being out on a call—and afterwards pulled into the long, winding drive that led up to the Broughton's clapboard farmhouse around 1:30. It wasn't apparent if anyone was home although an old '69 Chev sat outside the dirty blue clapboard garage.

The hood felt cold to the touch, not that I'd expected it to even be in working order. I checked the backyard but got no hints as to the whereabouts of the occupants. It told me a lot about their penchant for neatness though—totally lacking.

A couple of outbuildings to the right of the garage partially obscured my view of the vegetable gardens, field, and forest behind this haven. From what I could see, there weren't any living creatures around, two-legged or otherwise.

Observation is just part of this job, however, so I trudged up the rickety front steps of the house and knocked on the door. Several times. Long enough to confirm my earlier assumption. A check of the garage came up empty, also.

One final possibility—two really—were the small barn-like structures. The first, with door conveniently hanging open on one hinge, turned out to be a large tool shed with everything from a riding mower to hoes and rakes.

There was a narrow space between the two structures, barely wide enough for the assortment of discarded and decaying farm implements stuffed there. The gleam of chrome caught my eye, top right-hand corner. I worked my way around to the back, conscious of what might be lying in wait, slithering or standing.

In fact, it was parked. The chrome outlined the windshield of a white Dodge panel truck, probably about fifteen years old. The side view sported the name, Broughton Bros., Kemptville, Ont. And the zinger—a picture of carrots.

I crept up to the passenger door which turned out to be locked. In fact, the whole damn thing was locked. I didn't think they did such things in the country. The windows needed a cleaning before they'd reveal anything of interest or use. I wrote down the plate number for good measure then headed for structure number two.

The door creaked as I started to open it, which set off a series of peculiar sounds from somewhere inside. Damn close to fowl sounds, if you asked me. I took a minute playing with the phrase "probable cause" and decided to go for it. The "probable suspect vehicle" was parked out back, after all.

The inside looked like a storage area with bags of fertilizer, seeds, and grains. Tracking the noise to the far left corner, I encountered a make-shift three-quarter high wall of mismatched boards running the width of the room. By now the squawking had hit fever pitch with all the occupants pitching in.

The only thing worse than the noise was the smell. Shallow breathing was definitely called for.

I eased open the gate and got my first view of the white swans, either hoping for mealtime or agitated at being disturbed. I managed to close the gate before they hit it, but what I hadn't counted on was company.

The two men facing me, once I'd turned around, looked similar enough to be brothers—obviously the Broughtons. However, only one held a gun and it was pointed at me.

"Watcha doing here?" snarled the cowboy.

"Looking for some lost birds. Those are the missing Ottawa swans, aren't they?"

I indicated the noise behind me with a nod of my head. That also allowed me to scan the room for another possible out or, at worst, a place to duck in case this guy was serious.

His smirk answered that one, with chilling clarity.

"And what if they are? You planning on doin' somethin' about it, little lady?"

My height has never been an issue, except to these six-foot-plus, three-hundred-pound-plus felons. I considered my options. Very few, really.

"Isn't this overkill?" It just popped out. "I mean, walking off with several birds isn't a major crime, but holding a police officer at gunpoint is. And that's what I am . . . Constable Kellog with the Ottawa Police. Now, why don't you put away your weapon, we'll load the swans up in your truck and take them back to the city. Before things get out of hand."

The gun-toter laughed. "You don't know frig-all what's happening here. And you ain't going nowhere."

"Maybe she's right, Bubba." The weaponless one finally spoke.

"Shit, Kevin, she'd have us behind bars and throw away the key if she got the chance. Don't let the fact she's a piece of skirt fool ya. She's a cop, and you know what's waitin' for us once they get their hands on us."

Kevin nodded, probably something he was used to doing, following Bubba's lead.

"Look," I looked directly at Kevin, "why don't you tell me the whole story and I'll see what I can do to help."

He looked at Bubba who shook his head and waved his gun. Kevin repeated the head gesture in case I'd missed it the first time.

"I don't think so," Kevin informed me, stringing out the words into a sentence twice as long.

I pretended to be hanging on his every word but my attention had focused on a wooden handle protruding through the bales of hay piled behind the two lads. If it wasn't attached to something permanently imbedded in the floor, I had a chance. If I could waltz these guys around to where I now stood.

I tried talking and inching. "Listen, I can't believe you'd seriously take a chance on doing time for a weapons offence, plus obstructing justice, and unlawfully detaining an officer. That adds up to a lot of years." I held my hands up and let the fingers flick into view one at a time for Kevin's benefit.

Bubba had turned some of his attention to the swans and, the gun hand still covering me, was pushing open the stall door. I did a slight side-step when he peered in at the noise. Kevin obliged by sidling up to his brother. A couple of more moves like this and I'd be within grabbing range.

"God damn it, Kev, I thought I told you to muck out this pen right before lunch. Now we've got a full morning's crap to go through."

"I forgot," Kevin whimpered and pushed past Bubba into the pen, giving me a chance to relocate again. "I'll do it right now, Bubba. I'll do it all by myself. You'll see, I'll do a good job."

"Shit, Kevin. Watch where you're stepping. You could be crushing them."

Bubba let go and cuffed Kevin one across the head and I lunged for the stick. It pulled free with little effort. By the time Bubba realized I had a weapon, it had whacked him across the hand.

He screamed and backed into the pen, but held onto the gun. I struck again, this time aiming at a more tender, vital spot. Prong-end first. Right between his legs.

This time Bubba dropped the gun and followed it to the ground. He lay writhing in the muck, cursing at top volume.

The swans hissed their anger, flapped their wings, and went on the attack. Kevin stood in shocked silence.

I kept my eye on him, just in case, while reaching into the pen for the gun.

"Kevin." I had to yell his name several times to be heard over the ruckus. "Pull him out of there."

Kevin reached into the foray, grabbed an arm, and started pulling. The swans took a few well-aimed lunges at Kevin, then backed off once the bulk of Bubba's body was through the opening.

"Kevin," I shouted, "move over there." I waved the gun to a spot to the right of the pen where I could keep an eye on him.

He started to squat down near Bubba who had managed to prop himself against the wall. Bubba's growl was lost in the general bedlam still emanating from the pen but one look at his face had Kevin moving quickly to the side. Right where I wanted him.

By the time the noise level had abated, the outside door swung open, and my cute constable appeared.

"Renfrew to the rescue," I quipped, even though I had the wrong police force.

The constable—Greg Silver—took one look at the tableau and radioed in on his portable for reinforcements.

"You want to explain this?" Silver finally asked, trying to keep a straight face.

"I did check in with your detachment," I quickly informed him, "then came out to determine if six white swans abducted from the city of Ottawa were on the premises. They are."

I handed Bubba's weapon over to Silver, nodding in the direction of the pen at the same time.

"And I," he answered, "also checked in and was told of your visit. So tell me, Constable Kellog, are you formally charging these two as the perpetrators?"

He remembered my name. I smiled. "Yes, however, there are a few more questions I'd like to ask them."

I walked over to Kevin, blocking his view of his brother. "So, what's the whole story? Why go to all this trouble for six white swans?"

Kevin tried to peer around me but I was too quick for him. Finally, he gave up trying and talked.

"It's the stones."

This wouldn't be easy. "What stones, Kevin?"

Bubba growled but I heard Silver move and then silence. Kevin cleared his throat.

"You know. Those gems."

"What gems, Kevin?" My heart did a rapid two-step. Not the uncut gems of Brian Noble's robbery? Was fate this kind?

"You know, the ones in that heist. From that rich house."

Hallelujah. "And just how did you come to be in possession of them?" There's no way I'd believe these two had master-minded such a classy theft.

"My cousin, Martin, has a pawn-shop in town. Some guy brought 'em in and left 'em."

"Martin's a fence."

Kevin gulped and nodded.

"Go on."

"So, we were there when he came in with 'em and then Martin had to go out and asked us to handle things till he got back, so we pocketed the stones and left. Bubba called Martin to tell him we'd give 'em back for a cut of the money. Only . . . I'd gone to feed the birds and I guess, well, I musta opened the wrong bag. The stones went flyin' and the swans started eating 'em. There weren't none of the black ones around so's we only had to make off with the whites, don't ya see?"

I could heard Silver trying to stifle a vocal sound of his own this time while I tried to think of an appropriate response.

"We wouldn'ta hurt 'em," Kevin hastened to reassure me. "I wouldn't let Bubba kill 'em so we were waiting for 'em to shit out the stones. I'd never hurt a dumb animal."

Word had reached the office by the time I'd signed in my prisoners in the basement lock-up. Brian walked over and slid his case file on my desk.

"Thought you'd like to add your own report to this one." He winked and sat back down.

The sergeant muttered, "What dumb luck."

I waited to be summoned by the inspector. No summons, but she did give me a "thumbs-up" sign as she passed by my desk.

I pulled a "Robbery" report form out of the drawer and started filling in the top—my name, cadre number, date of occurrence, etc. The phone rang before I got into the subjective portion.

"It's Silver. Just wondering if you're free for supper tomorrow."

Be still my heart. "Sounds interesting . . . what did you have in mind?"

Pause. Which should have prepared me for what was coming. "How about I pick you up at six. I was thinking of someplace in Manotick."

Another clue, but what the heck. I knew I'd be hearing a lot more of these in the days, even weeks, to come. So I fed him the line he wanted.

"What place?"

"The Swan."

Light Spousekeeping

John Snell was quite a ladies' man,
So well turned out and trim,
Though I was only seventeen
I rushed to marry him.
But once he had me in his house
He lost his loving airs.
He wanted me to clean for him—
I pushed him down the stairs.

At eighteen I looked good in black,
And caught the eye of Jim,
A cowboy known as Gold Strike James,
So I latched on to him,
But his prairie home was just a shack.
A maid was what he needed.
Gold Strike James struck-out with me—
His docile herd stampeded.

This grieving widow found a mate
By name of Abd-el-Krim,
Who said he was an Arab prince
And would I marry him?

But when we got to Africa
I had to clean his house.
I was wife number thirty-one—
I stabbed the royal louse.

A freighter captain helped me flee
Aboard the S.S. Grimm.
He said I was a comely lass,
And so I married him.
But he made me clean up his mess
While he went out to sea.
The first day that he reappeared
I nightshaded his tea.

Of all the luck, they found me out,
I stood before Judge Brimm,
Who gave me five (he fell in love)
And soon I'm marrying him.
The judge has hired six cleaning maids,
He quickly has foreseen
That I do widows very well—
But I will never clean.

Joy Hewitt Mann

SERENDIPITY:

"THE FACULTY OF FINDING VALUABLE OR AGREEABLE THINGS NOT SOUGHT AFTER"

by Joan Boswell

Jane surveyed the crowd in Salon Four of Addison's Funeral Home. Half the population of St Ivan's School flowed through the tastefully decorated beige room. A host of young men shuffled in the door, signed the book of condolences, and moved along to shake hands with Nina's husband and exchange embarrassed hugs or handshakes with Nina's son. The students, in ill-fitting school blazers and grey flannels, avoided looking at, much less approaching, the open coffin. Instead, they quietly greeted friends, and, after a decent interval, sidled towards the exit.

Standing to one side with her friend Cathy Young, Jane decided the atmosphere reminded her of a public meeting where people came to see and be seen. Certainly, she'd come for that reason. Given the circumstances of Nina's death, Jane, who'd despised Nina, had felt it necessary to make an appearance.

"Quite a crowd," murmured a voice in her ear.

Jane turned. Merle Dorian hovered behind her.

"It's always a shock when anyone connected to the school dies. Especially mothers. Mothers aren't supposed to die." Jane's eyes narrowed. "The kids didn't know she was a bitch on wheels."

"You're supposed to speak kindly of the dead," Merle admonished in a whisper.

"I know I am, but it's difficult. To change the subject, did they ask you to testify at the inquest?"

"Yes. They want to hear from everyone working in the common-room when it happened."

"I didn't think they could bury the body until after the inquest. But I guess since they know she was electrocuted, it's okay."

"Do you keep thinking about that morning?" Merle asked.

Jane patted her friend's arm. "There was nothing anyone could have done. It was a freak accident, nothing more."

It had happened on Friday, November ninth, the beginning of the mid-term break and the busiest time of the year for Jane, president of the Ladies' Guild. Each year, on that weekend, the guild sponsored the Antique Fair.

On Thursday evening and all day Friday, with the help of the custodian's staff and some of the senior boys, the gymnasium, common-rooms, and classes were converted into showrooms for the Friday evening gala opening. Dozens of last-minute crises always arose. It was a madhouse, but the venture made thousands of dollars for the school. Although they never seemed to have enough volunteers, no one suggested giving it up.

Petit, perfectly groomed Nina Amalfi had been one volunteer who'd been more trouble than she'd been worth. Jane couldn't say she hadn't been warned. She thought back to the previous spring when the nominating committee had considered Nina's request to join the executive.

When Nina's name came up, Merle had twisted on her chair.

"I don't like bad-mouthing anyone, but if we accept her we'll have trouble."

"Can you be more specific?" Jane asked.

Everyone waited while Merle bit her lower lip, sighed, twisted again. Finally, she straightened her back and leaned forward.

"As some of you know, my third son, Stephen, backpacked through Asia last year after he finished grade thirteen. He came back sick; really, really sick. We were so worried. Our doctor didn't know what was wrong with him. He lost more weight and broke out in a terrible rash." She shook her head. "But you don't need chapter and verse. It turned out to be an obscure bacterial infection and Stephen did, finally, get better."

Merle paused and stared at us. "Later, I was told that Nina phoned people and warned them to avoid having any physical contact with Stephen."

Her lips tightened and her voice shook. "Ethel told me she confronted Nina and asked her what she was implying. Nina said SHE didn't want to imply anything, but Bangkok WAS the AIDS capital of the Far East." Merle slumped back.

Despite Merle's story, the executive reluctantly accepted Nina.

As Merle had feared, Nina, initially meek, mild, and helpful, soon stirred up dissent. Jane could think of many meetings when Nina, lips pursed in an insincere smile, touched someone's private sorrow or shame with a hurtful insinuating remark or an unanswerable allegation.

On one occasion, Jane found out exactly how it felt to be impaled on Nina's rapier. The executive had been discussing the information about university programs the senior students received.

"One thing we want to do is steer them away from inferior schools," Nina said. Her eyes widened. "Cathy, do you know what your husband told me last week at the sports day?"

A look of dread on her face, Cathy shook her head.

"He said the law course at the University of Southern Ontario is so inadequate, reputable corporate law firms won't hire the graduates."

Cathy's face reddened, but she didn't respond, nor did anyone else, although two sneaked quick glances at Jane. Nina, who'd been tapping her beautifully manicured nails on the table, looked around, patted her perfectly cut hair and managed to appear both smug and contrite.

"Oh Jane, I'm sorry. I'd forgotten your oldest son is in the program."

Jane smiled weakly and mumbled something about getting back on track.

At seven-thirty on Friday morning, standing alone in the basement common-room, remembering that day, Jane still felt annoyed. She shrugged and turned her attention back to the Antique Fair. The common-room's metamorphosis from a depressing place to leave empty coffee cups to a bright showcase for four dealers specializing in early Canadian furniture, clocks, miscellaneous collectibles, and antique garden statuary was nearly complete.

Savouring the quiet, Jane sipped a cup of coffee and consulted her list of things to do. The metallic click of heels descending the stairs ended her solitude.

Nina charged into the room followed by her son Cyrus who carried a large cardboard carton topped with evergreen boughs.

"Jane, you saw the wonderful fountain Pat Mossman brought in last night? The one with the three smiling fish spouting water over the tiny little frog holding a clutch of lily pads over his head as an umbrella."

"Mmm." Jane knew she was about to hear something she didn't want to hear.

"I'm rigging it up with a circulating pump. I talked to Roger Smith's father and he's sending in an aluminum horse trough with Roger this morning." She pointed to the box Cyrus held. "We've brought a hose. Cyrus will connect it to the tap in the custodian's cupboard. And he'll cover the tank with the greenery."

She leaned towards Jane, who wondered what it would be like to deliver a neat right hook to Nina's jaw. "Cyrus will rig up lighting so we only see the fish."

It sounded reasonable. If only it wasn't the morning of opening day, when Nina had promised to do other things.

Nina spoke as if responding to Jane's thoughts. "Martha is going to drive around and collect the sherry the embassies are donating. And Cyrus will do my kitchen detail after he finishes helping me here."

Looking at the perfectly groomed Nina, Jane reflected sourly that Nina always managed to avoid doing anything grubby. Poor Cyrus. Nevertheless, to be fair, Nina had commandeered others to do her jobs.

"Well, I suppose since you've got it all arranged, it'll be okay." Jane hated herself for being so wishy-washy, but what else could she say? At least Nina wasn't stirring up trouble.

Nina, who hadn't waited for Jane's grudging approval, directed Cyrus to move tables and other furniture to make way for the fountain.

In the next few minutes the room filled with volunteers and dealers. Nina didn't offer to help anyone. Instead, she waited, tapping her nails on the fountain, until Roger Smith and a helper appeared. She stood by while Cyrus and the other two struggled down the stairs lugging the enormous container.

With the trough in place, Nina directed a sulky looking Cyrus to elevate and balance the fountain on a table behind the trough. After he connected the hose and turned it on, she sent him, feet dragging, to the drama department to get spotlights to position over the fountain.

Jane managed to keep half-an-eye on things from the other side of the room where she was replacing a key volunteer felled by flu. She crawled about on the floor laying electrical cords and taping them securely to the floor.

Two volunteers organized a sherry table where media celebrities would dispense "bon mots" and liquid cheer. Merle draped white sheets over the tables as the collectibles dealer began unloading boxes of trays. Cathy, tiny and busy as a hummingbird, unpacked and made last-minute changes to a pile of signs before she began climbing cautiously up and down a ladder attaching dealers' names above the tables and rigging signs directing patrons to the sherry table, the upper hall, the snack bar, and the washrooms.

Nina waited until the fountain was filled before she turned on the circulating pump.

Even though it had forced the nearby dealers to crowd closer and blocked part of the aisle, Jane grudgingly admitted to herself that the fountain looked attractive burbling away in the nest of pine boughs. Nina unplugged the pump and spoke to Cathy who knelt on the stairs sticking signs saying MORE ANTIQUES UPSTAIRS to each riser.

"Cathy, I'm taking the ladder to put up the spotlights."

She didn't wait for Cathy to reply but dragged the ladder towards the fountain display.

The two who'd been setting up the sherry table walked towards the door.

"Throw the switch for the power out in the hall. I'm going to put these spots up, and the wiring looks old." Nina ordered, directing her remarks at the backs of the sherry ladies.

As if nobody else needed power. Jane gritted her teeth and finished anchoring the cords under the clock-seller's booth. When she straightened up, she realized the display of Thirties electric kitchen clocks continued to hum. Mickey Mouse swung his gloved hands around the dial. A Dutch windmill's arms rotated.

Jane glanced around to see if anyone else had noticed and locked eyes with Merle who stood in front of the collectibles table holding a large tin tray. Merle immediately looked away. Jane turned to see Cathy sit back on the top step of the stairs and point to the ladder. Nina had her foot on the second rung. "Nina, be careful of . . ."

A metallic crash as Merle dropped the tray on the concrete floor drowned out whatever Cathy had been about to say.

In the next five seconds, Nina, clutching the frayed wires and the spots, climbed three rungs of the ladder. When she stepped on the fourth rung, it gave way and she pitched into the horse trough. The wires hit the water. An arc of electricity jumped through the air. Nina screamed. Everyone else froze.

Standing at the back of the funeral home, Jane again patted Merle's arm reassuringly. Of course, it had been an accident. The two who left the room had not realized Nina was speaking to them. Cathy had been about to warn Nina about the fourth rung of the ladder when Merle dropped the tray. Of course, Merle hadn't meant to let it fall. Jane hadn't had time to tell Nina the power was still on. And, who could have known that Nina's son had taken the frayed extension cords and the defective lights from a box about to be consigned to the dump. How to explain what had happened? Serendipity, that's what it had been. Good old garden fountain serendipity.

SECRETS OF THE NIGHT

by Barbara Fradkin

The moment I heard the phone, I knew I was in trouble. I was supposed to be on back-up, which means the worker on call only phones me if she's desperate. And who else would it be at this ungodly hour? My head told me it had to be ungodly even before I could decipher my watch.

Ah. Two-seventeen.

The witching hour for the families who were my stock-in-trade. The hour when Daddy, just home from the bars, decides to wake the little woman up for some fun and games. Or Mummy, stoned on crack and dressed in lace and spandex, decides the party's over and tries to kick that night's pick-up out of her bed. Or Mummy and Daddy, both pissed to the gills, start throwing pots and knives around the kitchen at each other. And four-year old Mikie gets in the way . . .

Do I sound cynical? At two-seventeen, after twenty years with Children's Aid, I get like that. But I try not to let it show. Following the sound, I finally tracked the phone down under the half-read paperbacks on the couch.

"Marilyn!" A breathy voice burst through the wire. "Thank God! I was afraid you weren't there."

Where else would I be, I was tempted to reply. Lolling in satin sheets with my Latin lover, the latest in an endless stream? But she sounded way beyond light banter.

"Beth? What's up?"

"I've been called in on a case and I really need you. I've got a house full of corpses and a kid who won't come out from under the bed. No one talks to kids in shock better than you."

It was nice to know, after years of slammed doors and fuck-yous, that someone thought I was good at something. But at two-thirty in the morning, facing a house full of corpses, it was scant comfort. My pulse was racing as I drove through the deadened streets.

It was a muggy Wednesday night in July, and my T-shirt stuck to my back after two blocks. The address Beth White had given me was in one of the public housing projects in Ottawa's west end. Some bureaucrat had decided years ago that lumping all the city's poor together in one place would be more efficient. Cloned strings of cheap townhouses clad in brown brick and khaki siding were clumped around squares of grass or parking lots. Paint peeled and weed gardens flourished.

I'd been here many times over the years. In fact, the first seeds of my cynicism had been sown here, on this very block, fifteen years ago. That time too, it had been the middle of the night when a distraught mother had called for my help. I could only hope this time there'd be a happier ending.

Normally, tricycles and children's toys cluttered the strip of grass along the fronts, and teenagers skateboarded in and out between the parked cars. But tonight, at almost three a.m., the scene was out of a movie set. Throngs of half-clad people milled in the streets, drawn by the sirens, the red flashing lights, and the eight or ten official-looking vehicles clustered at the curb. Yellow plastic police tape enclosed the entire front yard of a townhouse in the middle of the row. Half a dozen uniforms held the crowd back, stolidly ignoring all questions.

Although cops rank better than lawyers on my jerk list, my experience with them hasn't been especially enriching. In child and family welfare matters, most of them have the sensitivity and insight of cannon-balls, and about the same subtlety. Setting my jaw, I marched forward prepared to do battle. I'm a formidable sight with my jaw set; at six feet even in flats, with a shock of iron-grey hair and ice-blue eyes, I can play chicken with the best of them. But in fact the patrolman barely reacted when I waved my CAS card under his nose.

"Oh, you're supposed to go inside. They'll tell you at the door where to walk and what not to touch."

I had been steeling myself for this moment since Beth's call. Because she had been on the verge of hysteria, I hadn't asked for details and I wasn't sure what to expect as I eased open the door to peer inside.

The interior was alive with lights and people. Blank paper squares dotted the floor. White-coated crime scene cops crawled about, flashes popped, and cops snapped orders back and forth. I was just about to step inside when I heard a roar.

"Watch the blood!"

I froze, scanning the room. A grey-suited lumberjack with his tie tucked in his shirt was rolling towards me, waving his arms. Then I saw the blood.

Sprayed on the walls, dolloped on the floor, splashed in the kitchen and trailing across the hall up the stairs out of sight. Still wet and glistening in some places, dried to almost black in others.

I'm not the squeamish type; I've seen my share of bloodied children and battered wives. But the blood, and the tale it told of panic and desperate flight, chilled me with horror.

"CAS?" the lumberjack barked.

I nodded brusquely to overcome the horror..

"The kid's upstairs under her bed. Jammed right in the corner, way out of reach. We could have dragged her out, but . . . "

Nice of you to restrain yourself, I wanted to say, but professionalism won out. "Is she hurt?"

The cop shrugged, making his neck disappear up to his ears. Sweat soaked his collar. He had a bulldog's face, all jowls and beady eyes, and even his voice was a growl. Sergeant Peter Thompson, according to the ID on his lapel.

"Hard to tell. Won't say a word. All you can see is these eyes staring out at you."

"What happened?"

"We're still piecing it together. The call came in at one-oh-three, patrol car got here at one-ten. Found two bodies, white, male and female, in the master bedroom upstairs, throats slit. No one else in the house except the kid. Doors locked from the inside, front and back."

I scanned the room, noticing more subtle details now. The faded chintz curtain on the front door was ripped from its rod and dangled in shreds down one side. A lamp lay askew on the living room floor at the end of the hall, casting an eerie floodlight on the back wall and illuminating a broken vase which had scattered plastic flowers and shards of blue pottery over the carpet. In my mind, the panicked flight unfolded. She had fled across the living room, knocking over the lamp, and hurling the vase at him before scrambling towards the front door. She had clutched at the curtain as he dragged her back and locked the door on her escape. He had hauled her into the kitchen, where someone had got hold of a knife. Even as I thought it, I saw the container of kitchen utensils sitting by the sink. Spatulas, wooden spoons, tongs, and knives stood on end, easy to grab.

"Domestic murder-suicide?" I asked.

Thompson had been studying some illegible scrawl in his notebook, and his nod was distracted. "Looks that way. We got a file on this pair. Neighbours've called 911 a couple of times. We respond, place is trashed, wife's clothes are torn. But the guy's all remorseful, promises he won't drink anymore, and she says she walked into a door." He shrugged in disgust.

Since cops and I generally don't see eye to eye on things, even though we deal in the same human wreckage, I found it a bad sign that I was thinking the same thing he probably was—women can be such fools.

"I'll go see the little girl," I muttered to cover my irritation. "What's her name?"

He flipped through his notebook. "Crystal Leblanc, according to the lady next door who made the 911 call. Heard a hell of a lot of screaming. Nothing new, she said, only this time it went on longer than usual. Seemed to start up again worse than ever after she thought they'd settled down. Got her scared. Anyway, she says Crystal's about six."

"Anyone else live with them? Any other kids?"

"Looks like there's an older kid but no one else was in the house when we got here. I'm on my way over to interview the neighbours right now."

"Let me know if there are any other kids or relatives this child might be close to."

Thompson jotted in his notebook and nodded. "Step only on the paper squares, don't touch anything. Bedroom's on your left at the top of the stairs."

I followed the white paper squares, but they took me right into the master bedroom. The first thing I saw was the man's body, a scrawny reed sprawled in a pool on the floor, head flung back and chest a mass of red ooze. I gasped. Three men who had been bent over the bed spun around, revealing the woman's body. She was slumped over the edge of the bed, as fat as he was skinny, her head dangling and tendrils of sticky hair touching the floor. The room reeked of gin.

"You from the lab?" one man demanded.

"No. CAS." I retreated hastily across the hall.

Beth had been sitting on the floor and jumped to her feet with a cry as I burst into the room. She took my elbow and steered me back into the hall, pulling the door shut behind her. She looked pale, but then I probably looked green.

"She's still under the bed," she whispered. "I can't get a word out of her. Do you think we need a doctor?"

I shook my head. "Give me some time to try to reach her. Do we know anything about her or her family?"

"We have a file on the mother, Karen Monk, from ten years ago. It lists her and two kids, seven and eight. They're pulling the file for me right now so we can see what it was about."

"Two kids? But they'd be teenagers now. Where are they?"

Beth shrugged, then gestured towards the open bedroom beside Crystal's. "That looks like a teen-age boy's room."

A brief glance into the room revealed black walls hung with posters of heavy metal rock groups and a huge blood-red Nazi swastika over the bed. An open window rattled the blind and sent gusts of hot air through the room.

"Not the kind of teen-age boy I'd want around," I muttered. "I'd better see the little girl."

Silence greeted me as I entered her room, and I felt an eerie sense of deja vu. Fifteen years ago, in a room much like this one, I'd tried to reach another frightened girl, only that time she'd been in a closet. Eight years old but mildly retarded, she had barricaded herself in and refused to come out. Most of what I'd learned about frightened kids came from Jessica. In retrospect, she gave far more than she got in return.

I turned the bedside light on and shut the door, humming a verse of "Mary had a Little Lamb." The heat was stifling, and I felt sweat beading at my temples. Kneeling on all fours, I peered under the bed. At first I could see nothing, but gradually a huddled form took shape against the shadow. Huge dark eyes glowed in a cloud of pale curls. I tried for my gentlest smile.

"Hi, Crystal, I'm Marilyn. I shut the door so no one else is going to come in here. It's safe."

The huddled form did not move. I watched for a moment and the eyes never left my face.

"You want to stay in there a little longer? That's okay. You can stay as long as you feel like. I'll just sit out here with you, okay?"

Still nothing. I sat back against the wall where she could see me but I couldn't see her. I let the silence lengthen, hoping she'd relax. If you're calm and take your time with kids, they often come around.

"Are you scared, Crystal?" I didn't expect a reply; I was merely laying the ground for a speech. "I used to get scared when I was your age. I still get scared sometimes and then you know what I do? I go to my favourite place and find my favourite toy and I just hold it, really tight. I used to have a stuffed bunny named Munchie and he was really nice to hug. Do you have a special animal or doll you'd like me to get for you?"

As I talked, I glanced around. It was a little girl's bedroom, papered in pink flowered hats and sparsely furnished in a medley of Sally Ann and Zellers specials. There was a chipped chest of drawers, a cast-iron bed, and a plastic doll's house in the corner, missing its roof. Barbie dolls were laid out in a neat array against the wall. Again I thought of Jessica and her collection of fancy dolls. Over the years I had added to it every birthday, just to see the smile that had become so rare.

"I see you have lots of Barbies. Aren't they fun? But not to cuddle. For that you need something that's soft, squishy, and smells good, right?" I rose and walked around the room to check for stuffed bears or tattered, much-loved blankets. I moved slowly, not wanting her to feel spooked or violated. If she was an abused kid, then this room might be her private sanctuary, and the corner under the bed her only safe haven. I didn't want her to see me as an invader. Her bed was an unmade jumble of sheets and blankets, and as I began to paw through these, I heard a faint whimper. I stopped and backed away.

"I'm here, Crystal. It's okay." I picked up a brown teddy bear that had fallen off the bed. Holding it out, I knelt to look under the bed. Crystal had pressed herself even further into the corner.

"I found this teddy. Is he your special friend? Do you want to hug him?" I placed the bear under the bed near her. Without warning her foot shot out and kicked the bear across the room. Jessica, too, had been very angry at the toys her father gave her. It was one of the things I told the cops. 'That's evidence?' they had snorted. Yes, it was evidence to those who could see.

"I guess you don't want teddy. Is there someone else? This dog? Or this bunny?" I had found a cache of stuffed animals in the closet and I placed them in a row on the floor by the bed where she could see them. A minute passed.

"The bunny," came a very faint voice.

Hallelujah, I thought to myself, she's not dissociating. I'm in touch. I edged the bunny towards her until she snatched it up. As I sat back against the wall and waited, I could hear her rocking slightly. It was a touching sound. At a moment like this, the slammed doors, bureaucratic red tape, and judicial stupidity don't really matter anymore.

"Feels good, doesn't it," I ventured. "Not so scary any more. You're safe, sweetie. The scary stuff is all gone."

"I want my mummy."

Oh boy. "I know you do, honey. What does your mummy do to help you when you're scared?"

"Hugs me."

"That feels good, doesn't it. Does she hold your hand sometimes?"

"Yeah."

"Maybe it would help to hold my hand. Here's my hand—" I laid my hand down lightly under the bed, palm up. "You don't have to take it, but you can if you feel like it. I won't pull you or make you come out, I promise. I'll just hold your hand."

A minute passed and my hand began to grow numb, but she didn't move. In the silence, I could hear soft rustling of paper on the stairs. The lab guys would be taking samples of every bloodstain and stray fibre, piecing the facts together bit by bit until they knew exactly who had done what to whom. Not why. The "Why" didn't count for much in the court-room.

"My mummy's dead, isn't she."

I barely missed a beat. "Yes, honey. I'm afraid she's dead."

"And Daddy too?"

Here I faltered. I believe in telling children the truth, but this much truth? "Daddy too."

"And Mel?"

"Who's Mel?"

She said nothing.

"Mel—is that your brother?"

I could hear her breath quicken, but she remained mute. I tried another tack. "Nobody else is dead. Mel is not dead."

"But she ran away."

"Oh, did she?" I replied, flying blind. At least I knew Mel wasn't the brother. "When? Tonight?"

"Who's going to take care of me?"

I was used to this. Kids often veer off on tangents when feelings get too intense. In some of my interviews with Jessica, she had flitted around the room, bouncing from topic to topic and mixing fact with fantasy in a vivid stream of consciousness. It was one of the things that made the judge unsure. "A reasonable doubt," he had said from up there on his pedestal, with his half-glasses and neat white hair. "After all, she was slow and it might be hard for her to distinguish truth from supposition or, say, sugges-tion." As if kids can tell you, in clear and objective facts, the story of their own rape.

So I followed Crystal where she needed to go. "Do you have a grannie or grandpa, or an auntie?"

"They're far away."

"Do you know where they live?" For a six-year-old, far away could be Russia, or it could be across town.

"On a farm. They don't like Mummy."

"Well, that's okay. Does your mummy have any special friends who take care of you sometimes? Anybody you really like?"

"No. Only—" She broke off.

"Only who?"

"Daddy doesn't like strangers to take care of me. Strangers might hurt me. And Mummy says the people around here are bad."

Part of me felt triumphant. Although my hand lay numb and empty beside her, she had said three whole sentences! But the message in them was ominous. Were her parents just lovingly overprotective, or trying to hide some sinister secret from outside eyes?

"How about your brother? Does your brother still live here?"

There was a silence, then a small voice. "No."

"Would you like your brother to come here right now?"

She made a little noise that sounded like a moan. I couldn't interpret it but I had to talk to the cop to obtain more information, so I pushed away from the wall.

"Okay, honey, I'm going to get up and go out for a moment to—"

Abruptly she pounced on my hand and clutched it to her. Despite the heat, her hand was cold. Cradled in mine, it trembled slightly.

"It's okay, honey. I'm right here."

We sat in silence until gradually her hand began to grow warm.

"I want Mel," she whispered.

I stirred. "Okay. I'll go tell the policeman downstairs to find her. Then I'll come right back. I promise."

She hung on tight.

"I'll send Beth back in, and bunny will stay with you."

Slowly, very slowly, her fingers loosened and I extricated my hand.

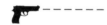

I found Sergeant Thompson interviewing the neighbour in the town-house next door. Mrs. Black, an overweight woman in a floral nightdress several sizes too small, wheezed around the kitchen getting me cookies and lemonade for as long as she dared before Thompson chased her out. He was jack-knifed behind her kitchen table, sweating over his notes, and slurping lemonade.

"Kid say anything?"

I picked up the cold glass of lemonade. "She knows her parents are dead."

"She say how?"

I bristled. Nice of you to ask how she's handling it, I thought. "It's too hard for her to talk about. I don't want to push her."

"Yeah, but we got two dead bodies and—"

"And a child this close to the edge. I'm not pushing her over."

"But there's some things that don't add up, and the kid may be the only one who can make them."

"What doesn't add up?"

"The doors were locked from the inside—deadbolts, so you have to be inside to lock them."

"But that supports the murder-suicide theory," I countered. "No one else was in the house."

"Yeah, but the murder weapon's got no prints on the handle. Looks like someone tried to wipe it off. Hard to do that after your throat's slit."

I raised an eyebrow. "You think someone else broke in, chased them around the house, and slit both their throats?"

I suspected I was irritating him but his voice stayed flat. "I can't rule it out. Not till the kid tells me different."

"But how did this person get out afterwards?"

"A window was open upstairs."

"And you think he jumped? From the second storey?"

Thompson shrugged his by-now-familiar world-weary shrug. "It's been done before, ma'am. For crimes a lot smaller than murder. I got Ident checking the ground. An impact like that should leave marks."

I thought about the open window in the bedroom next to Crystal's, and all the rage the room expressed. "Who's Mel?" I asked suddenly.

Thompson's eyes narrowed. "Probably Melanie, the half-sister. I got men looking for both older kids. Why do you ask?"

"Crystal asked if she was dead too."

"Melanie doesn't live with them, according to Mrs. Black here. She's eighteen, moved out two years ago. Turned sixteen and—zap, hit the streets."

"She ran away?"

"Mel was always running away." Mrs. Black, who had apparently been hovering in the hallway behind the door, could no longer contain herself. She plopped her considerable bulk down at the table, sending up a whiff like rotting lilies. "Her and Guy could never get along. Karen, bless her, tried to keep the peace but her two older ones—they weren't Guy's—they just never accepted his authority. Fought him every chance they got. Finally this past month, Guy kicked Jason out altogether. He's living in some hellhole with his pals pushing drugs, most likely. If he ain't in jail."

"Did he ever mention getting even?" Thompson asked her.

"Oh, plenty. He'd come back looking for money or something to steal, they'd get in a huge fight, threaten to kill each other, and then Jason would stomp off."

"Did you see him today?"

She shook her head. "Not him. Just Mel."

Thompson's head snapped up. "When was she here?"

"Sometime this aft. But Mel's straightened herself around now. She's back finishing school and working at a bank. Her and her mom are on good terms and she visits often. Babysits Crystal for them. She's been trying to help Karen get on her feet, upgrade her education and get a decent job. Karen's from one of them small valley towns and her folks kicked her out when she got pregnant. She's been wanting to move out of this neighbourhood and find a better place to raise Crystal, so she won't turn out like Jason. 'Course—"

"What time was Melanie here?"

Mrs. Black patted her face dry with a kitchen towel and picked up a chocolate chip cookie, dropping crumbs onto her large frontal shelf. She crunched, head cocked, as she considered the question. "Well, that's the funny thing. Usually she comes when she knows Guy's going to be out, because she still hates his guts. But today I'm sure she came just after four. She knows Karen works two to eight most days and Guy's home taking care of Crystal. But that's when she came. Didn't stay, though. Stormed back out of there not three minutes after. Must have had one of their fights."

"Did you see anyone else visiting the house later on in the evening?"

"Well, 'course I left for bingo about seven, got back at eleven, so I wouldn't have seen anything. Fell sound asleep till the screaming woke me up."

I wanted to ask more about Jason but remembered the little girl waiting for me under the bed. Trust is a fragile thing for a child like that, and to her ten minutes would seem like desertion. So I poured her a drink and left the cop to handle Mrs. Black.

Beth collided with me just as I moved to open Crystal's door and she gave an exclamation of relief. "She was starting to ask about you. She wants you to find her older sister."

"I know. The cops are looking for both kids now. By the way, did you find out why we had a file on the mother?"

Beth nodded. "And it was very interesting. The family doctor called in a report of suspected sexual abuse based on his annual physicals of the children. We interviewed both Melanie and Jason, as well as the mother and stepfather, but got nowhere. Flat denials across the board. We left the file open for awhile, but since there was no other evidence to go on . . ." She sighed, but did not finish. There was no need.

"Who was the victim? Melanie?"

"Both kids. This guy wasn't picky."

"And off the record, did the worker have a suspect?"

"The stepfather. Guy Leblanc."

Crystal took my hand very readily when I extended it to her. We sat together in silence awhile as she drank her lemonade. I hummed a nameless Raffi tune while I sorted through the pieces in my head.

"Sorry I was away so long, Crystal. They're looking for Melanie now. Okay?"

"Okay."

"Did you see Melanie when she came here this afternoon?"

Crystal jerked her hand back and rocked fitfully. Half of me tried to figure that out while the other half wondered what to say next.

"Did Jason come over today too?"

"It's my fault." Her voice was a bare whisper.

"What's your fault?"

"Mummy and Daddy are dead."

Kids' logic can be awfully screwy from an adult perspective, so I knew I wasn't listening to a murder confession. They spice up facts with a dash of omnipotence and magic. A wish, a thought, a feeling—in a child's mind they can all cause events to happen. You wish Daddy was dead, presto he's dead—so you killed him. Kids take on so much guilt for the awful things adults do that sometimes the guilt can crush them.

"You know," I launched into another of my hokey speeches. "Sometimes we get mad at people, really mad, and we wish they'd go away, or even die. But that doesn't make it happen. Wishes don't really come true, Crystal, like in fairy tales. Someone else killed your daddy and mummy. It was very scary for you, but it wasn't you chasing them around with the knife."

"But Mummy was so mad. Because of me. Because I did bad things."

Ah—another twist in the trail of a child's logic. Jessica had thought it was all her fault too. The trial, the divorce, the custody battle . . . The judge's access order was merely her punishment, carried out every weekend for ten years. Until she lost her mind.

I probed to follow the twist in the logic. "Mummy was mad at Daddy?"

I heard a faint whimper under the bed and Crystal began to rock again. Her hand clutched mine.

"They had a big fight. She wanted to go away."

"You mean she wanted to go away from the house? From Daddy?"

"Daddy got so mad. He broke the lamp."

"What did you do?"

"I ran up here. I always run up here when they fight."

"Scary, isn't it."

The rocking intensified. I debated my next move. I was afraid to push her but she finally seemed to want to talk, so I tried for a middle ground. "We can talk about whatever you want, honey."

Unexpectedly she began to cry in soft, sibilant whimpers. I tightened my grip on her hand, wishing I could pull her into my arms.

"What's making you sad, sweetheart?"

"My Daddy killed my Mummy, didn't he."

"I don't know. Did he?"

"They were fighting and she was screaming, and I heard them run upstairs. Then they stopped. Daddy started crying. I was so scared. Then—"

The door creaked open, making me jump, and Thompson stuck his head in.

"Anything?"

I wanted to rip his dumb head off, but settled for the most ferocious glare I could muster. I released Crystal's hand with a reassuring whisper and shoved him out into the hall.

"I was just getting the story, you idiot. I told you, this is very delicate. This little girl has just witnessed both her parents being murdered. She's six years old. She's alone and she's terrified, and more than anything she needs to feel safe!"

"But did she tell you anything?"

I gritted my teeth. Once a lunk, always . . . "Yes. It sounds like the father killed the mother because she was going to leave him."

"Yeah, well I figured that much. The knife fight started in the kitchen, both their blood is in there and on the stairs. Coroner says the wife died about half an hour before the old man. But just so you know, the sister Melanie came back later that evening. One of the neighbours saw her about nine. Came in and had a screaming match with her mother and left again. The neighbour heard stuff like 'You never knew because you never wanted to know' and 'If you don't do something, I will.' Sounds like a threat to me."

All at once the pieces fit together. I knew why Melanie had come that afternoon, and what she had seen. "He was molesting Crystal, you know. Maybe Melanie just planned to inform the authorities or take Crystal away."

"Maybe she planned that, but found her mother sliced up in the bedroom, and—"

"But Melanie's been trying to straighten herself out. Besides, she's all the little girl's got."

Thompson seemed to ponder that. His face was beet-red, but perhaps it was just the heat.

"Yeah?" he growled finally. "Well, I got partial footprints and a broken bush under the window at the back of the house, but nothing I can use, so I need to know. The kid's got to tell you."

I went back inside with a heavy heart. I wanted no more part of this. If Melanie had killed her stepfather, who could blame her? Justice is rendered in many forms more perfect than our legal system, but the big lunk outside could never be that subtle.

Crystal was shaking all over when I reached for her hand, and I wondered if she had overheard. "Crystal," I crooned. "I know you're scared. Do you want to come out here beside me so I can hold you tight?"

Crystal loosened her grip and for a moment I thought she was going to retreat. Come on, sweetheart, I begged silently. Don't give up. Fight. You've got to fight for yourself in this life. Like Melanie's been trying to do. Maybe if Jessica had fought back, she wouldn't be staring at padded walls.

In the silence I could hear shuffling and murmuring out in the hall. They were moving the bodies out. Just as I was looking for new words to help her, and me, the little girl stirred. Slowly she slid forward until she laid her head in my lap. Wordlessly I drew her to me and rocked her. I couldn't have talked anyway.

"Melanie said she'd come back." Her voice was muffled in my shoulder. In my dismay, I stopped rocking, but forced myself to resume. Don't tell me any more, I wanted to say but I couldn't, for Crystal needed to talk. Perhaps at least I could steer her towards more innocuous ground.

"You like her, don't you."

"She plays Barbies with me, and she takes me to the park. And tonight I was going to have a sleepover at her apartment."

I dodged adroitly. "What about Jason?"

"Jason's mean. He yells at me and he slaps me on the head when I'm bad. Mel never yells at me."

"Sisters are great, eh?" Inane, but safe. Or so I thought.

"She said she'd take care of me. Always. She had to run away when the police came but she said she'd come back to get me."

Oh God, I thought. There it is. The lunk was waiting to see justice done, but what was justice for Guy Leblanc, after all? Death by his own hand, in a drunken fit of grief and remorse—that was justice. It had symmetry, closure, and this time the children would win.

Fifteen minutes later, when I was sure the bodies were gone, I led Crystal out of the room. Thompson looked up expectantly as I brought her down the stairs.

"She doesn't know anything more."

"No, eh?" Thompson eyed her pinched face and her hand clutching mine. Then his eyes met mine and I thought he nodded, ever so slightly. That was all.

And just for an instant, I wondered if he knew.

Gender Bender

Miss Marple is charming

Warshawski's disarming

(a felon who got in her way),

Jenny Cain is a saint,

But Di Palma sure ain't

(in fact, she's a little risque),

"Cat" Marsala is thinking

Kat Colorado is sinking

her claws into her "terror"tory,

But whoever the sleuth,

ain't it the truth,

we women create quite a story.

Joy Hewitt Mann

THE DEWEY DECIMAL MURDER

by Victoria Cameron

Miffy Tome knew it would be a memorable day in Maudlyn Mills as soon as she turned the corner.

The car parked in front of the Maudlyn Mills Public Library faced the wrong way. The driver's door hung open over the sidewalk. Like someone was desperate for a book. He or she had sprung out of the car and rushed into the library, with only seconds to spare. He or she must have been arriving from another time zone. The library was about to open, not close.

Miffy smoothed the chain of pearls attached to the arms of her half-glasses. He or she would just have to wait until the librarian and the proper hour arrived.

She walked past the lilac bushes lining the library lawn, and turned up the path, expecting to see someone in urgent need of a good book anxiously stamping his or her feet at the front door.

He or she was a he. He was not waiting at the door. He was slumped against the book return box, one arm caught in the Deposit-Books-Here drawer.

Miffy stopped. Mr. Bordnoff. No doubt attempting a hit-and-run return of his overdue books. Caught in the act. Probably trying to jam all thirty-seven of them in at once. The tipping drawer must have seized up under the weight, trapping his arm.

"Well, well, well, Mr. Bordnoff," she said. "Trying to avoid the fine, are we? This won't look good on your library record, you know."

Mr. Bordnoff said nothing, no doubt overcome with shame.

"I'll see if I can help you out." She stepped to the rear of the box and opened it with her key. "I expect a cheque to cover the fine, though. Do I have your assurance on that point, Mr. Bordnoff?"

No reply.

She opened the back of the box. Yes, there they were, at least thirty-seven books. Big coffee-table books. The entire 635 section. Books from the top of the best-seller list. At least, they had been at the top when he had borrowed them. Now they were relics.

She sighed. "This is not an auspicious moment in your library career." He said nothing.

She looked around the box, at his face, jammed against the dark-green metal. He was quite white, his pallor no doubt influenced by his caved-in skull and the little trickles of blood seeping down his forehead.

She decided against touching the wrist dangling in the box. There could be no doubt. He was quite dead.

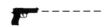

Miffy stood beside Sergeant Flack and watched the team of policemen string a long yellow tape around the library property, including the lilac bushes. Police Line. Do Not Cross.

"Does this mean I won't be able to open the library on time this morning?" she asked.

Sergeant Flack flipped open a crisp black notebook and poised a crisp black pen over the crisp white page. "Not today at all. Maybe not tomorrow, either."

"Not open? I'll have you know, Sergeant, this library has never failed to open. Of course, we were slightly delayed on June 2, 1953, because of the Queen's coronation."

"Think of this as a longer delay, then." He tapped his pen on the page. "All right. This is my case. I'd like to ask you a few questions. Are you the librarian?"

"Yes."

"Are there any other librarians on duty today?"

"Jennifer Swallow, my volunteer assistant, helps on Saturdays."

"Is she here?"

"Not yet. Not until ten. She watches television before she comes to the library. She's taking a course, you see."

"What time did you arrive on the scene?"

"Eight o'clock."

"The library opens at eight?"

"No, at nine on Saturdays. I realize you're a newcomer to Maudlyn Mills, Sergeant, but you ought to be more familiar with the public library. Our hours are one to nine p.m. on weekdays, nine to five on Saturdays, closed Sundays."

"I'm not a newcomer. I've been here a couple of years."

"Seventeen months and three weeks. You have visited the library twice."

"So?"

How could she explain this to a man from the city? There were certain sacred institutions in Maudlyn Mills. The Library, the Volunteer Fire Department, the Patron Ladies, the Historical Society, the Maudlyn Mills Community Choir, the Maudlyn Mills Fair Board. To be truly part of the fabric of the community, one had to belong to one or more of these, and be in good standing. To do less was to remain an outsider, a person classified as "no use to the community." She could not explain that in twenty-five words or less while swarms of police officers buzzed around them. She pursed her lips. Let him seek his own answers to the mysteries of Maudlyn Mills.

He drew a line in his book. "All right. This . . . ," he pointed at the busy scene on the library lawn, " . . . is my case. Why were you here early?"

"I always come an hour early, to make sure everything is in order before the public hours start at nine o'clock."

"And you found . . . "

"I found Mr. Bordnoff trapped in the overdue book box. I opened up the back to help him free his arm. That's when I noticed he had passed away. At least he returned his books first."

Sergeant Flack did not look pleased. "Are these books important?"

"In this case, yes. He had thirty-seven books out. Our entire collection on lawn bowling, lawns, gardens, homes with gardens, and balls. Plus a number of light reading books, those with historical settings and mention of gardens. I only wish he had enclosed a cheque. He owes the library $397.40 in overdue fines. He reached our fine ceiling months ago. We're a small library, Sergeant. We can't afford to replace entire Dewey sections of books. And we can't afford to gather a reputation as an institution which doesn't enforce its own rules. We have our status in the community to uphold. At least he won't be withdrawing any more books."

Sergeant Flack wrote in his notebook with tiny perfect letters. One of the other policemen stepped out of the lilac bushes with a large clear plastic bag.

"Sir? Possible weapon here."

Sergeant Flack took the heavy bag by the top, held it up, and rotated it slowly. Miffy could see bits of hair and blood mixed with dirt clinging to the brown ball.

"Recognize this, Miss Tome?"

"Yes, I do. It's a Dewey Decimal. 600 to 699. Applied Science."

"Hmm. Looks more like a five-pin bowling ball."

"In a previous life, yes. The bowling alley donates retired balls to us. Those no longer fit for service. They seem to have a few ruffians at the bowling alley, and so they have a reserve of chipped and cracked balls. We paint the numbers on them, and use them as visual aids to explain the Dewey Decimal System. Youngsters like that, you know. Visual aids."

Sergeant Flack handed the bag back to the officer. "Check with the neighbours. See if anyone saw anything."

"Yes, sir." The officer returned to the other side of the yellow line. A moment later, he was off down the street, notebook at the ready.

Sergeant Flack turned to a fresh page. "And who paints the numbers on the balls?"

"My volunteer assistant, Jennifer Swallow. She paints the little scenes on them, too, depicting the nature of the number. Biography, Literature, Language, History. Applied Science had a wonderful collection of engineering and scientific instruments. Microscopes, slide rules, callipers. You must have noticed the fine artistry. I'm sure you are well acquainted with the Dewey Decimal System, Sergeant. Although I don't feel you use your library card as often as one would hope." She glanced at the policemen huddled over the evidence bags. "I don't suppose I could rinse that decimal off and reshelve it?"

Sergeant Flack gave her a dark look. "Not while this is my case."

Dear, dear. Poor Jennifer's hard work gone for naught. She would have to make another Applied Science.

The sergeant tapped his notebook. "Where are the rest of these balls?"

"We keep them in a trough in the children's section. Or at least, we try. They're quite popular. We have a problem with shrinkage. It's amazing what children can cram into their knapsacks."

"And had this particular one disappeared?"

"I'll have to check the records. Jennifer and I count them frequently."

The neighbourhood-searching officer appeared again, with a Dewey decimal in his hands. He was accompanied by an angry young woman dragging a scruffy child. "Sir? Found another one."

The woman gave her son a little shake. "Throwing them at squirrels, he was. Trying to kill squirrels."

Miffy looked a the ball. 921. Individual Biography. A portrait of Louisa May Alcott. Another ball Jennifer would have to redo, she suspected. The officer was already bagging and tagging it.

"This is my case," Sergeant Flack told the woman. "Have a seat in my car. I'd like to talk to you."

Another officer stepped over to the Sergeant. "Sir? Time of death fairly recent. Coroner wants to speak to you."

Miffy nodded. "Yes, I thought he looked quite fresh."

Sergeant Flack closed his notebook and frowned at her. "Don't leave town," he said, and walked away to join the clot of officers huddled around the book box.

Miffy watched the woman and her son being escorted into the back seat of a police car. Throwing Dewey decimals at squirrels. Had a squirrel been bounding through the lilacs when Mr. Bordnoff made his Kamikaze pass at the book return box?

She checked her watch. Almost time for Mrs. Pendleton-Smythe to make her routine Saturday morning visit to the library. Since she couldn't open the library and do her job, she should wait and explain the situation to her best customer. Possibly accept her returned books, too.

Mrs. Pendleton-Smythe marched down the sidewalk bang on schedule, 9:31, her books tucked under her arm. She raised one eyebrow at the sight of the librarian standing on the sidewalk, and frowned at the yellow police line.

"What is the meaning of this?" she asked. "Is the library closed?"

"Sadly, yes. Mr. Bordnoff passed away."

"I fail to see why the library should go into mourning. Especially for a reprobate like him."

"He died on the library steps. The police have to tidy up. But I can take your books."

"Good." Mrs. Pendleton-Smythe dumped her burden in Miffy's arms. "So, we won't have that man to cope with anymore. Good. Pig-headed and unreasonable if you ask me. He was in that wretched lawn-bowling club. They're nothing but a sorry collection of renegades. We in the Historical Society were gearing up for our annual elections. We were to have a panel discussion on local historic homes. She who knows her history gets elected president of the group. Everyone knows that. And when I went to do the research, guess who had all the books? He wasn't using them, mind. He was just keeping them out of circulation. On purpose. Claimed he was doing a paper for the lawn bowlers. His selfish actions caused me to lose the presidency. I told him, right there in the express line at the grocery store, 'I'll have your head on a platter for this.' He said it was his right to use the public library. Insufferable cad."

"You might want to tell this to Sergeant Flack. It's his case."

"That interloper? What does he know about life here? Nothing. He has no idea how important a Historical Society position is. None at all."

Mrs. Pendleton-Smythe turned on one heel and marched away. Miffy stared. How much was the Historical Society presidency worth? In dollars, nothing. In prestige, plenty. She who headed the Historical Society ruled the town's higher society. Mrs. Pendleton-Smythe didn't have many more years to compete. Had she been angry enough at Mr. Bordnoff to make him pay for her loss? How many witnesses had heard her make a death threat?

She put the returned books in the trunk of her car, and drove around the corner to Jennifer's basement apartment.

A distraught Jennifer answered the door. "Oh, Miss Tome. Come in. My class. Still on."

Miffy held up a hand. "Carry on, Jennifer. I'll wait until it's finished."

She settled herself on Jennifer's couch and picked up a newspaper from the end table. The Maudlyn Mills Review. Jennifer hurried back to her armchair. On the television, a gentleman in a plumed velvet cap talked at length about the joy of sixteenth-century poets.

Miffy had seen this programme before. The Joy of Books. An educational programme screened by low-budget cable companies. Jennifer was dedicated to becoming a community success, if unsure how to become one. Born and raised in Maudlyn Mills, she had never left it. She wasn't brave enough to move to the city and attend college. Instead, she filled her head with a thousand useless bits of information, in the hope they would become useful some day. She gathered random college credits by mail and by instructional television. Seven years of Video Academy.

Notes and stacks of books flooded her coffee table. Her key to the library perched on a pile of texts. Her Saturday mornings were totally devoted to bettering herself.

Miffy pursed her lips. Jennifer needed more than books and quasi-credits to get ahead in Maudlyn Mills. She needed a nod from someone like Mrs. Pendleton-Smythe, and an appointment to the Fair Board. Jennifer was balanced on the peak of a watershed. Look good to the right people and slide into the ruling faction. Slip the wrong way, and be forever doomed to dally in unrespectable organizations like the lawn-bowling club.

The Joy of Books theme music welled up. Jennifer made frantic notes as the scene faded.

Miffy folded her newspaper precisely. "Jennifer, you needn't hurry away from your studies. The library is closed for the day. Possibly tomorrow, too. I shall call you when we can resume operations."

"Is something wrong?" Jennifer's pen paused in mid-stroke.

"Yes, Mr. Bordnoff has passed away. In front of the library."

Jennifer sighed and laid down her pen. "Oh, dear. What a shame."

"Yes. I suppose one could call it a shame." Miffy nodded. "Not a popular man, though. Especially in my books. His misuse of library property was appalling. He totally disregarded his First, Second, Third, and Final Overdue Notices. I wondered if he had even received them."

"Yes, he got the final one all right," Jennifer said, snapping her books shut. "He came to the library one evening, and waved it in my face. He yelled at me, in that loud voice, about how it was his right to keep his books over the time limit, and how we had no right to expect money from him. Public money and public books for public use, he said. If we didn't waste our funds on frivolous items like the Dewey Decimals, we could meet our budget without having to resort to charging our customers for minor infractions."

"Minor indeed."

"I was so embarrassed. He went on and on. If we had wanted the books, why hadn't we phoned him and sent someone to pick them up? We were never open at convenient hours. How could we expect him to return the books?"

"You didn't tell me this, Jennifer. As librarian, I must be made aware of incidents such as these."

"How could I tell you?" Jennifer sighed again. "I lost my standing in the community. The Historical Society was meeting in the Reference Section. They heard everything he said."

"Oh, dear. That could be quite damaging. What did you do?"

"I cried. Right there in the library. I cried." She shuddered.

Miffy clucked and shook her head. Wrong response, when Mrs. Pendleton-Smythe was in the room. She liked forthrightness and spunk.

"How can they ever consider me for any position in this community?" Jennifer asked of the books spread on her table. "The Historical people are the Community Choir. Most of them are Patron Ladies, too. How can they think me fit for office? I'm nothing, now. I'm finished."

She straightened her books into a neat pile. "At least we got his books back. I'll have to go and get another Decimal, though, and make another Applied Science."

Miffy patted her on the shoulder and left. Poor humiliated Jennifer.

Well, let Sergeant Flack figure it out. It was his case.

WITH FRIENDS LIKE THESE

by Sue Pike

Dotty had always considered herself an extremely fortunate person until that morning in February when somebody tried to kill her.

She had a lovely home, devoted friends, and the best husband anyone could hope for. She knew her friends envied her. That knowledge had always given her a keen satisfaction. But now, studying the plastic thread stretched across the basement steps, she realized she would have to reassess her position.

Luckily, Adonis had gone first down the dark stairs. He came out of the fall with little more than an injured look on his perky Pekinese face. But his tumble and Dotty's scream had alerted the other members of the bridge club and there they all were, looking rather silly, she thought, as they pushed and squeezed against one another in the basement doorway.

Annabelle's bulk took up most of the space. "What in the world has that dog done to you, Dotty?" Having to rush made her wheeze.

"Oh, Dotty, what happened? You frightened us half to death. We thought you'd fallen." Helen Jane's voice croaked from a chronic sore throat. She clutched at the strands of orange and lime green beads hanging around her stringy neck.

"My dear! Are you all right?" Mabs poked her head around Annabelle's elbow, her eyes large and anxious behind their thick lenses, her scalp gleaming pinkly between thinning strands of pale blue hair.

Dotty almost blurted out about the thread, but looking up at her friends, she realized if someone had intended her to fall it had to have been one of them. Who else had been in the house in the last few hours? Only them, her very best friends. The thought was extremely galling.

"I'm fine. But Adonis has had a tumble. He may be hurt," Dotty said, picking up the dog and carrying him back up the stairs. "I think I'll have to take him to the vet's immediately."

Adonis was squirming to get down and looked none the worse for his tumble, but Dotty needed time alone to think.

"You go ahead then. We'll finish the game next week at my house." Annabelle was already on her way to the vestibule to get her coat. "Everybody remember that Dotty and I are vulnerable."

I'll say, thought Dotty, shifting the dog to one arm in order to help Mabs get into her mud-coloured parka. The fabric was so worn at the sleeve ends that the feathers were poking through.

Dotty went out to the verandah to see them off. Mabs turned to wave as she climbed into Annabelle's rusty old Buick and a cloud of goose down wafted to the ground. In the February cold, Helen Jane's nose was turning a mottled red. She dabbed at it with a wad of tissue and sank into the front passenger seat. Annabelle's old camel hair didn't quite stretch to meet across her middle. She tugged at it as she struggled to get behind the wheel. All three of her friends were looking tatty, Dotty thought, shivering slightly and wrapping her blue cashmere cardigan across her bosom. How had she failed to notice it before?

The women had been friends since 1963 when the four young families had first moved into Trembling Aspens, a brand-new suburban development on the outskirts of Ottawa. The aspens, if there ever were any, had fallen prey to bulldozers and for the first year or two it was like living on the face of a particularly muddy moon. The wives kept themselves sane by having coffee at one another's houses while the children made loam statues of one another.

Now, as she looked down Merriweather Avenue and around at the gracious neighbourhood she and Lofty had moved to twenty years ago when Daddy had died and left her just enough money to purchase this house, she gave a sigh of contentment. She and Lofty had certainly fared better than the other three couples. Theirs was also the only marriage to survive intact. The other husbands had all taken up with younger women. Well, not all, she amended. Annabelle's Ted had had that fatal encounter with a snowplough on the Queensway several years ago.

Dotty carried Adonis inside and dumped him on the floor of the vestibule. She plucked a pair of scissors from the oak rack in the kitchen, turned on the basement light and picked her way down to the fifth stair from the bottom, watching for other booby traps along the way. Dotty cut the piece of plastic filament from the rung where it was still tied in a triple knot. The other end was attached to the paneling opposite by a copper cup hook.

She carried everything upstairs again and laid them out on the kitchen table. This would require a fresh pot of tea, she thought. Brandy might be therapeutic, but Dotty had purged the house of alcohol several years ago, after Lofty retired and became too dependent on his evening tipple. She filled the kettle and thought about calling Lofty. He often had lunch with his cronies—old fishing buddies or colleagues from his working days. Today she had volunteered him to work at the church rummage sale. She could probably catch him there but it was hard to imagine what she might say.

Guess what, dear? One of my best friends is trying to kill me. No, she had to figure out who it was first, and why in the world she was doing it.

Dotty made the tea and set it on a doily in the centre of her best silver tray. Sliced lemons and milk were already in the living room on the tea trolley, along with the Chelsea buns she had served just before making her unfortunate trip down to the recreation room to get the latest photos of her grandchildren. She collected the trolley and settled into a kitchen chair. Then she took a stack of blank index cards from her recipe file and began to think about the other accidents.

The first time she had felt even the slightest niggle of uneasiness was a month ago after a pot luck luncheon at Annabelle's. Dotty's contribution had been a dozen fresh oysters on the half shell. It had completely slipped her mind that none of the others would eat oysters. They often made a fuss about food allergies and Dotty couldn't be expected to remember every little whim. She enjoyed the oysters enormously but became dreadfully ill within hours and, as Lofty was still out, had to ask a neighbour to take her to the hospital.

Dotty wrote: Annabelle's—oysters—poison, on one of the cards.

She smiled as she thought about what a lovely nursemaid Lofty had made during her convalescence, fetching and toting without a hint of complaint. Dotty adored the little silver bell that would draw him from the farthest reaches of the house to plump her pillows and refresh her water glass.

The second incident had occurred only last week. She'd been to Mabs' flat to drop off some clothes she had grown tired of. Mabs hadn't wanted them at first, complaining they would never fit her small frame. Dotty had been forced to insist and the whole visit had taken longer than she intended. By the time she left Mabs' poky little apartment to go home, it was already dark. While she was still half a block away, she spotted the bus pulling up to the stop. She put on a modest burst of speed but arrived just as the bus began to pull away. Suddenly she felt a sharp push on her shoulder and found herself falling. Luckily the bus veered away and she only suffered a bruised knee. As she picked herself up and turned to look behind her, she thought she saw a mud-coloured parka disappearing behind a hedge at the corner. At the time she put the accident down to hooligans, the kind of riff-raff that would be likely to live in such a poor neighbourhood. Now she wasn't so sure.

Dotty wrote: Mabs'—push—bus, on a second card.

After studying these cryptic messages for a moment she turned her attention to the plastic thread that Adonis had tripped over.

It was too thick for dental floss but there was a similar feel to it. Where had she seen thread like that before? Suddenly she remembered. Helen Jane's neck was festooned with it. It was beading thread. It had to be. Helen Jane was always making some awful necklace or other. Horrid, cheap beads that looked like eyeballs or worse. Helen Jane couldn't leave them alone, always tugging at them until the string broke. She would stand there crying and trying to catch the wretched things as they tumbled to the floor.

On a third card Dotty wrote: Helen Jane—beading thread—stairs.

It began to appear that each of her friends had the means to kill her. The question remained, why?

Dotty wrote: Motive? on a fourth card. She worried the pencil around with her teeth.

What possible motive could anyone have for trying to kill one's best friend? Dotty pondered the question but she kept coming up with the same answer. The motive had to be Lofty. Lofty and the beautiful house, of course. Perhaps she had boasted too much about Lofty's amenable nature, his willingness to concede on any point to keep the peace.

Could any of her friends be foolish enough to think Lofty might marry her if Dotty was dead? If the thought of someone trying to kill her wasn't so frightening, it would be laughable. Whoever it was obviously hadn't realized the depth of Lofty's devotion. He would be inconsolable, and certainly none of these homely old cats would be able to tempt him out of his mourning.

If only she could be sure which one of her friends had decided on this murderous route to happiness. She looked again at the cards lined up in front of her. The only person who could have taken part in all three incidents, she decided, was Mabs. Mabs was forever complaining about squirrels getting into the bird feeder on her balcony. She must have bought some kind of rat poison and then put it on Dotty's oysters. Dotty remembered now that Mabs had spent some time alone in Annabelle's kitchen. Putting together the salad, she had said.

And who else knew Dotty was going over to drop off the old clothes? Dotty had told Mabs she would be travelling by bus because her own car was in the shop. Mabs must have waited for Dotty to get ahead of her and then put on her own coat and followed her to the bus stop.

Today's incident was a little trickier. How would Mabs get hold of Helen Jane's beading thread? Dotty frowned and drummed on the tabletop with her nails. Suddenly it came to her. The last time Helen Jane's beads had scattered was at that same luncheon. Mabs had offered to go to Helen Jane's house the next day to help re-string them on the pretense that she wanted to learn how to do it. She could have helped herself to some extra thread then.

Dotty sat back and massaged her temples. She felt her heart pounding with an old familiar rage. She hadn't felt this angry since she was twelve and cousin Timmy had caught her and pulled her panties down in their grandmother's barn. She'd stopped Timmy with a pitchfork. Even though they'd sent her away for a year to that special clinic, she had never felt much remorse. Timmy had to be stopped.

Dotty pulled herself together. She couldn't let Mabs get the better of her either. It was unthinkable. She was going to have to stop her as well.

Down in the basement, Dotty found her father's skeet-shooting gun hanging in the old gun case. It was a small pump-action shotgun, with an accurate range of about forty-five yards. Years ago Daddy had taught her how to clean it, load the shells, and fire it. She gave it a quick oiling and then stuffed it into a green garbage bag and carried it out to the garage along with some shells and Lofty's khaki hunting jacket and cap. Dotty stowed everything she would need in the trunk and then checked her little Cartier wristwatch. Annabelle would have had plenty of time to deliver everyone to their homes by now.

There was a lane behind Mabs' apartment building lined with old wooden garages and sheds. Dotty nosed her BMW into a spot behind one of these, then opened the trunk and pulled on the jacket and hat. She carried the plastic bag with the rifle and shells into one of the disused sheds. It took her a while to load it and line up the sights with Mabs' balcony. She left the gun leaning against the shed window, then got back into the car, and dialed Mabs' number on the cellular phone.

"Mabs, dear. It's Dotty. Remember that darling little garden chair I loaned you for your balcony? Well, I find I'm going to need it after all and I'd like to come by now to pick it up."

There was a pause. "But Dotty, you said it was mine to keep. I don't remember anything about a loan." Mabs' voice broke.

"Well, now I need it back. I'll be there in a few minutes. Please have it down at the front door so I don't have to climb those awful stairs." Dotty disconnected the phone and went back to the shed.

Dotty made sure the sights were lined up and then had to drum her nails for another five minutes before Mabs finally appeared. She looked pale and upset and instead of carrying the chair inside, she picked it up and heaved it over the balcony. Dotty was furious. She pulled the trigger and Mabs flew back against the balcony door before bouncing to the railing and pitching over it, following the path of the chair to the paving stones three stories down.

Dotty removed the coat and hat and gathered up the spent shell casing and the gun. She pushed the lot into the garbage bag and threw the bag into the back seat of the car.

"Of all the nerve. What was she planning to say when I arrived for the chair." Dotty muttered to herself as she pulled out of the laneway.

She was relieved to find that Lofty was still out when she got home, giving her time to put things back before he came home for supper.

The uproar over Mabs' death was predictable. Neighbours reported having seen teenagers hanging around the sheds on earlier occasions. There was a frenzied call for stiffer gun-control laws to keep firearms out of the hands of drug-crazed youngsters. Helen Jane was devastated and developed pneumonia before the week was out. Annabelle made the arrangements for the funeral and asked Lofty to be a pallbearer. Dotty made an appointment with the hairdresser.

It was the evening after Mabs' funeral that someone nearly succeeded in killing Dotty. She was on the Queen Elizabeth Driveway, only exceeding the speed limit by twenty kilometers or so, tapping her nails on the wheel in time to Rita MacNeil and watching the skaters gliding back and forth under the canopy of coloured lights strung along the shore of the Rideau Canal. Suddenly there was a jolt and the shriek of metal on metal. Dotty was thrown forward with such force that her head banged into the windshield. The little BMW veered into the guard-rail put there to stop cars from tumbling onto the skaters twenty feet below. Dotty had only a vague impression of an old blue car passing her and speeding off as her own car shuddered to a stop against a concrete post.

So it hadn't been Mabs after all, she thought as she rubbed the swelling coming up on her forehead. The only person she knew with an old blue Buick was Annabelle. And although it was ludicrous to think that fat, homely Annabelle fancied her chances with Lofty, it was serious business and had to be stopped.

"Annabelle, dear." Dotty called her first thing the next morning. "Lofty and I are going to the Manotick Tea Room for lunch today. We'll come by and pick you up. As our guest, of course."

"Can't. Already busy."

For someone who was ready to murder for the man, Annabelle was certainly playing hard to get.

"Oh, but you must. I have some good news about Mabs' will." It was a hastily thought-up lie but Annabelle swallowed it.

"Humph. Well, maybe I can rearrange my appointments," said Annabelle.

"Lovely. We'll come by around 11 o'clock. Could you wait for us on the road? You know how Lofty hates searching for a parking space."

At 11:20 Dotty spotted Annabelle and started up her car. She had parked behind a white van, half a block from Annabelle's duplex. Her anger increased with every minute she was kept waiting.

"How dare she," Dotty fumed as she stepped hard on the gas. "That's the last time we invite her anywhere."

Annabelle was ridiculously easy to run into. She made such a big target. The only unsettling moment was when their eyes met through the windshield just before she bounced off the hood.

Poor Helen Jane had never properly gotten over the pneumonia that she caught after Mabs' death. The blustery weather at Annabelle's interment finished her off completely. Lofty barely had time to get his morning suit cleaned before he had to don it again for Helen Jane's funeral.

Dotty snuggled up to Lofty as they drove down the long winding drive through the cemetery. She felt warm and safe at last.

"Oh Lofty. My very best friends. All passed away." She decided a tear or two would be becoming.

"Passed away?" Lofty seldom spoke and, when he did, Dotty quite often listened. "They're dead, Dorothy."

"Well, yes. Technically. But that makes it sound so final."

"Didn't you intend it to be final, Dorothy?" Lofty never took his eyes from the road. "Surely permanency was what you had in mind when you killed them."

"I? Why Lofty, how can you say such a thing?"

"Dorothy, my dear. Next time you decide to shoot someone you should tidy up after yourself. Oily rags. Shell casings in the pocket of my fishing jacket . . ."

"Well. perhaps. But surely you don't think I had anything to do with Annabelle. How could I know she'd be out on the street at that time." Dorothy was sitting up straight now, trying to catch Lofty's eye.

"Dorothy. Dorothy. Annabelle called after you left to say she was going to be a little late."

"Well then, Helen Jane? You can't think I had anything to do with that."

"No. Not Helen Jane. I think she probably died of a broken heart."

Dotty sniffed and let her head fall back onto Lofty's shoulder. "I had to do it, Lofty. They were trying to kill me."

"Kill you? Those silly old biddies? Don't be ridiculous."

"But it's true. One of them even tried to murder me on my own cellar stairs."

Just remembering it made Dotty angry all over again.

"The fishing line? That was only meant to put you out of commission for a while. If I'd meant it to kill you, I would have put it at the top of the stairs, not down near the bottom."

"Lofty? Are you telling me you tried to make me fall down the stairs?" Dotty was sitting bolt upright now, breathing hard. "And what about the oysters? That accident on the Driveway? And the push under the bus?"

"The bus was a spur-of-the-moment thing. So was the car, really. I thought perhaps a bruise or two. And there was only a little Ipecac on the oysters, Dorothy. Just enough to keep you in bed for a while and out of my hair." Lofty was silent for a moment. "You see, I need more peace and quiet, Dorothy. More time to pursue my own interests."

Dotty didn't like the little smile playing over his pursed lips. "All those accidents were your doing, Lofty? But you made me kill off all my friends."

"Yes, that was unfortunate. But friends can be a nuisance. Always checking up on you, seeing how you're doing." Lofty pulled the car into the driveway of the beautiful house on Merriweather Avenue.

Dotty gasped when she saw the man in the yellow blazer pounding a "For Sale" sign into the lawn.

"Lofty. What in the world . . ."

"I appreciate your putting the house in my name, Dorothy. And I know you would never dream of trying to revoke the offer. The newspapers would have a field day with the stories of your best friends—and your cousin Timmy, of course."

"Cousin Timmy?"

"Your father told me about that little incident just before he died. Wanted me to keep an eye on you in case your temper ever got the better of you again."

Something was wrong with Dotty's voice. All she could manage were small bleating sounds.

"I've already put an offer on a nice winterized fishing cabin up near Golden Lake. It should meet my needs exactly." Lofty paused and smiled at Dotty.

"Oh, I realize it's far too remote for you, Dorothy. You wouldn't like it at all. But guess what? I made a few calls and discovered Mabs' flat is still available. You'll be able to move in there immediately."

"It's a dirty job . . ."

He squeezed down the chimney,
Getting filthy and rank.
He struggled through the opening
To get into the bank.
They found him next morning,
In complete disarray,
Wedged tight in the ductwork,
Proving grime doesn't pay.

Joy Hewitt Mann

THERE GOES THE NEIGHBOURHOOD

by Linda Wiken

She just appeared one day, out of nowhere, or so it seemed.

"Hi, I'm your new neighbour. Christa Morgan."

I gave the topsoil around the newly planted azalea a final firm pat and looked up at the visitor, shading my eyes from the glare of the sun.

Her legs seemed to go on forever. Not an auspicious introduction to my 5-foot-2 frame.

"Hi, I'm Carolyn Brooks," I acknowledged, managing to stand up without the usual cracking of bones.

I still had to look up for a view of her face. Deep, blue eyes obviously enhanced by contacts. Flawless skin, probably coaxed by daily Estee Lauder routines. Thick, long auburn hair which had to have help to reach that shade. I'd keep an eye on the roots over the next while, to be sure.

"Welcome to Lake McGregor," I managed to get out. "When did you move in?"

"On the weekend."

That explained my missing the action. We'd been visiting friends in Oakville through Sunday.

"Sorry to interrupt your gardening," she went on, "but I thought it might be a good time to introduce myself."

"That's okay. This is my only effort at outdoor work and I've just finished. The bush was a birthday present from my husband."

"Oh. Happy birthday. Azalea, isn't it? He must be quite a romantic."

I hadn't thought of Doug as such, but she could be right. I invited her for a glass of iced tea, hoping to pump her for her life story, but she had to get back. She did say she painted for a hobby and had been letting the wash on the canvas dry. Time to move to phase two. I watched her svelte body weave through the overgrown path between our two places and vowed to resume my abandoned race-walking program that very day.

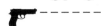 – – – – – –

I quizzed Doug about her that evening as we sat with our tea on the back deck.

"Really, the only thing I heard from the agent was she's single, has a government job in town, and likes solitude."

"So, why didn't you tell me?"

He shrugged. "I guess it slipped my mind. You know there's only one person around this lake who draws my attention." He reached over and squeezed my hand.

A romantic, indeed.

I filled him in on our short encounter and wondered aloud why an attractive, single, forty-three-year-old woman would buy a house on a lake by herself? Why would she choose to make the forty-odd-minute drive, twice a day, into Ottawa to her job and back? Especially during the sometimes treacherous winter days that lay ahead.

Maybe it was none of my business, Doug suggested. Ah, but the writer in me couldn't leave it alone. I felt a plot coming on.

I knew our reasons for choosing Lake McGregor well enough. I, as a writer, thrived on the daily solitude while Doug could cope with the drive. Or so he'd assured me the day we made our decision to buy the fully winterized three-bedroom bungalow. We hadn't bothered updating our thoughts on the subject in the four years since that signing.

"I really am intrigued by her," I said once more, giving him the opportunity to throw in whatever ideas he might have on the subject of her arrival. After a few minutes of silence, I added, "I wonder who might know more."

"Why not ask Millie-the-Mouth?"

"Of course."

Our self-appointed community oracle was back for the summer season but I'd been avoiding her protracted conversations. With a purpose in mind, though, I could sit through anything she could dish out.

Doug left for work at his usual early departure time the next morning and I took a brisk walk followed by four hours at my computer. This novel, number four in the series, was like writing the first one all over again. It just wouldn't come easily. Probably a good sign, considering how little effort went into the two in between, which showed in poor sales.

After a light lunch, I trekked down to the end of the cul-de-sac which was our arm of the lake, bearing a McCain's frozen chocolate cake, Millie's favourite.

"Oh, Carolyn, my dear. It's soooo good to see you. How was your winter? Get a lot of writing done? Not too lonely out here, was it? Did you keep an eye on my house, like a good girl? I've had the most fabulous time at my place in Arizona. I'll put on the tea pot and we'll have a nice cosy, girl-to-girl chat."

I could abandon all verbal skills when with Millie. The effort was in trying to feign interest and decide when to nod or to make sounds of agreement.

After a month-by-month recital of her winter, I decided to steer her towards my goal.

"By the way, the Rankin house sold and we've got a new neighbour."

"Yes, dear. I know. Christa Morgan. So unusual, a pretty young thing like her wanting to live alone up here. Why do you suppose that is?"

I'd hoped Millie would answer that one so I shrugged. "I guess she likes solitude. She says she's a painter."

"Only as a hobby, I suspect. She's some director or big-wig with Supply and Services, I hear. Guess that's why she could afford that outrageous price the Rankins were asking. I'm amazed they got it, but they say there's a buyer for every house. Talk is, she's got a boyfriend living at the other end of the lake, whichever end that is. And depending on who you talk to, she either lived with him last year or at the hotel, trying to see if she could take a winter up here."

I smiled and sipped while Millie continued.

"She'd probably make a good character in one of your stories."

"You're right. At least, if I knew why she was here. Of course, that part I could invent. But who knows, her story may be just as interesting as any I could create."

Millie put her cup down and reached for a second piece of cake, extending her body even further over the coffee table towards me.

"Maybe she's a drug dealer or something like that."

"At Lake McGregor? Who's her clientele?"

Millie looked offended. "Why, folks at her office, of course. This is where she hides out."

I didn't want to alienate my source. "Intriguing idea. I could work on that. Any others?"

She smiled. Millie likes being consulted. "Running away from her rich, old, overbearing husband? Or maybe she's kidnapped her child from her ex-husband who has custody and is hiding him out here. But, who'd take care of the kid while she's at work?" She shook her head. "Guess not."

This was a fertile imagination at work. I encouraged her to share several other ideas, none of which gelled, but could possibly be worked into a future plot.

"Oh, I've got to be going, Doug will be home soon. Good to have you back, Millie."

"Well, you just come over whenever you need a break. You know my door's always open."

And your mouth, I thought. But I meant it as a compliment today.

My story continued to plod through several more days of pages and revisions until a knock at the door interrupted my working morning. I toyed with the idea of pretending no one was home, but realized the red Samurai sitting in the drive gave me away.

Millie burst in as I eased open the door. "I'm sorry to bother you, dear, because I do know it's your writing time. But I had to share with you what I learned about Christa Morgan."

My annoyance gave way to curiosity. I knew Millie would take up the scent once I'd introduced it. Pay-off time was near.

I settled her into a lawn chair on the deck, while I poured us each a tall glass of iced tea and nuked some frozen over-sized chocolate chip cookies. Millie sighed at the sight of the tray I put in front of her. She reached for a cookie and had it almost finished before she started talking.

"Well, about Christa. I was over at the Harrison's last night—they always have me over for a barbecue as soon as they come up—and Ken Harrison had been talking to the realtor who sold the Rankin house. They—the Harrisons—had been thinking about selling but decided to wait another year. Prices are sort of low this season and they're not in any rush. Anyway, the agent told them that Christa paid cash. Can you imagine? That supports the theory about crime connections, doesn't it?"

I gave it some thought. Intriguing, although there could be any number of valid reasons, I supposed.

"What's your best bet, Millie?"

A pleased look flooded her face. "Well, dear, I think her boyfriend's that bar owner from Hull who built that monstrosity of a cottage around the bay a few years back. You know the talk is he deals in drugs and prostitutes. He probably bankrolled the buy. Talk was, he planned to use his house as a bordello for special clients. Maybe he'll get Christa to handle that end. What do you think?"

My creativity hadn't stretched that far. I looked at Millie with new-found respect.

"Interesting possibility. Quite probable, I'd guess. Except I haven't seen any activity over there. She drives a white Camry and so far that's the only car I've noticed."

"Well, she's still setting things up, dear. Getting the place ready. That's probably what she's painting. The rooms. Or maybe doing erotic pictures on the ceilings." Millie's eyes twinkled. She was getting a real charge out of the possibilities.

"I think I'll take her a McCain's chocolate cake this weekend. What do you think, Carolyn? Would she like that? She'd have to invite me in and I'd sneak a quick look around when I use the washroom."

"Go for it, Millie."

And she did.

Meanwhile, Doug had given up on me and my search for Christa's past. In fact, he grew damned touchy about the subject, even though I pointed out how I'd worked her into my new book. As the murder victim.

I'd liked Millie's latest theory so much, I'd adapted it, and Christa was being immortalized as Amanda Blais right on those pages. If I stared out of the window in my home office long enough, I could visualize the float plane landing on the lake and taxiing up to Christa's dock. Interestingly enough, those were the same days that Christa's Camry never left the driveway.

I'd spent several days going back to the beginning of the manuscript, revising, weaving my new victim throughout the plot with the result being a much happier writer. I'd mastered the slump and was well on my way to a commercial success. I hoped.

Millie appeared after lunch on Monday, waiting till she knew Doug was back at work and I had finished mine for the day. This time I thawed chocolate brownies for her.

"I had a look around but I'm afraid I don't have much to report," Millie opened with, then stuffed half a brownie into her mouth.

It didn't matter. I'd created my own material and Christa Morgan's true story seemed almost anti-climactic at this point. But, not to Millie.

"She has a couple of paintings on the go—landscapes—and one that's kept covered. I wanted to sneak a peek but thought I might be taking too much time. You know the bedroom in the top right corner, overlooking the lake . . . that's her studio. Looks like she's planning to put in a skylight. Lots of lines on the ceiling. Anyway, she seems really nice and she liked the cake. Invited me to stop by anytime, although she suggested I call first, just to make sure she wasn't painting."

Millie looked at me expectantly. I wasn't sure what to say. It sounded like a logical enough request to me.

"Well, that was good detective work on your part, Millie. I think I'll let my imagination fill in the gaps. Did you know that the Laval's daughter got engaged over winter?"

That got her started on her second favourite topic . . . matchmaking. She speculated about the other children who'd grown up spending their summers at the lake, wondering who'd be next to say, "I do." I let her work her way through the names I knew, then suggested I'd walk her home and continue on my route for the day.

"By the way, I have to go to Toronto for a couple of days. Tomorrow," Doug said at dinner that night. "Will you be okay?"

"Of course. Do you want a lift to the airport?"

"No. I'll park the car out there. How's the book going?"

"Nearing the end. I may use these two days to work round the clock. Try to finish it off."

He looked pleased. "Atta girl. It's all flowing again, right?"

"Yes. All it took was some inspiration."

I lay awake part of the night trying to come up with a clever way to kill off Amanda, my victim. My subconscious finished the job, as it often does, and I awoke with anticipation.

By dusk, I'd done the deadly deed and planned to spend the next day going over the story from the beginning, planting clues and red herrings along the way.

I noticed Christa's car was missing when I went to bed and still not there the next morning, too. Maybe I could work that in at some point. Build up the tension.

Another productive day at the keyboard gave way to a night of fitful sleep. My dreams centered on Amanda's death and by morning I knew I needed a break from my work.

As I savoured my morning's coffee on the deck, I realized Christa was still away. A desire to peek through her windows overwhelmed me and a few minutes later, I had cupped my hands on both sides of my face, nose pressed to glass for a view of her living room.

Nice furniture. Modern. Expensive. Same with the kitchen. No need to worry about being seen as a nosy neighbour. The only other house at our end of the bay was empty during the week. I continued to snoop with a tingle of delight.

Checking out the bedrooms was more difficult. The windows in the back afforded a partial view of the master bedroom, but no such luck with her studio. I turned the door knob, trying to remember if the place was alarmed, and gasped as the door eased open. I searched the wall frantically but couldn't spot a control panel. I tried calling out, in case she was home with the car in for repairs or something. But no answer. So, I walked in.

A quick tour of the house assured me there was no alarm system which I'd inadvertently triggered. My story to the cops would have been one of concern for a neighbour I hadn't seen in a couple of days. Especially with an unlocked door in the scenario.

The house was totally empty. No Christa, alive or otherwise. A mystery writer's imagination always thinks the worst.

I returned to the entry and took the stairs two at a time to the studio. The room was just as Millie had described it, right down to the covered painting. I approached it hesitantly, then lifted up the corner of the grey cloth. A male's naked torso took shape, in intricate detail, leaning back against a deck railing, cocky as hell.

I pulled the cover totally off and faced Doug.

I don't remember leaving the house, nor walking back to my own. I found myself sitting in the living room, scotch in hand, tears in my eyes. I toasted the air, wishing them a horrible trip wherever they were.

When Doug returned the next evening, supper was on the table, a smile on my face, and no mention made of my devastating suspicions.

I finished working on my novel over the next two days, entertained Millie through one gruelling afternoon, and got through the weekend by concentrating on domestic chores and my weekly Saturday shopping trip into town. Doug did a lot of work out in the yard, cutting back the under-growth that had separated our two houses over the years. I had to admit to him, he'd done a great job. Christa appeared on her deck at one point and waved to us, but didn't invite us over.

As I came back from my walk on Monday morning, I noticed Christa's car still in her driveway. It was still there a couple of hours later. Maybe she'd taken the day off and was working on her painting.

I took a chance.

She was surprised to see me when she answered my knock, but invited me in. I followed her out to the kitchen, which looked even more expensive as I sat there surrounded by the luxuries. What a pity. We made small talk—girl talk—as she turned on the gas stove to boil some water for tea. The pleasantries continued as we sipped it. I had an attack of the clumsies and spilled my tea, but Christa fetched a damp cloth before any damage could be done to her teak table-top. That gave me just enough time to drop the few grains of Catapres into her cup.

I left about half an hour later. Christa slept peacefully, at the kitchen table. I'd tried to make her comfortable. It had taken only a few minutes to pull the cord out of the telephone and cross the wires. The pilot light on the gas stove went out easily.

Back at my computer, I found the necessary page and blocked out the incriminating section about the fire, read the chapter over, and knew the story worked. I dialled Christa's phone number, then hung up as the windows in her house exploded outward. Flames were lapping at the roof by the time I called 9-1-1. It would take at least half-an-hour for the volunteer crew to make it out here on a workday.

We really should do something about that. I wanted to live in a safe neighbourhood, after all.

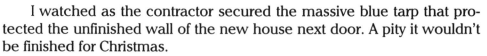

I watched as the contractor secured the massive blue tarp that protected the unfinished wall of the new house next door. A pity it wouldn't be finished for Christmas.

The microwave beeped me into action even though Doug wasn't home yet. Those late nights at the office were increasing again, much to my annoyance. But they wouldn't last for long. I glanced at the stairs then put the finishing touches on the special dinner I'd prepared to celebrate our ninth anniversary. The car pulled into the driveway and I dimmed the overhead lights and lit the candles.

Doug raved about my pork medallions with marsala sauce and the pecan pie, his favourites. He sat back with that smug smile he's mastered, sipping his brandy, as I opened the Howard's box and emoted about the sapphire earrings.

My turn next. I led him up the stairs, made him cover his eyes near the top, then steered him into the bedroom.

"Happy Anniversary, darling. Open your eyes."

I watched the horror spread across his face as he viewed the nude portrait of himself.

"I wanted to give you a gift that was meaningful."

COTTON ARMOUR

By Mary Jane Maffini

Cortés has been my model. He really knew how to make people toe the line. You have only to look at the size of his tiny Spanish force and the might of the Aztec Empire he conquered to grant him that. I owe a lot to his influence, up to and including, I must admit, the three years I reigned as President of the Parish League of Women. Three entire years at the top of the parish pile. A record for harnessing control and direction of the parish ladies who preferred to be let loose to wage their petty battles. I can see them now, gloating over their triumphs. How they loved to stake out tiny bits of turf: the altar flowers, the PLOW kitchen, the May procession, the Christmas pageant. But I had them all under my heel for three delicious years. That's right. Me. Don't you forget it.

And don't forget about my year as National Second Vice-President of the National Council of Parish Leagues of Women either. Me again.

That's right. Helen Denniger, Helen Mooney that was, whose mother was only a maid and no better than she ought to have been. That's the one. Helen Denniger, whose father was nothing but a drunk, if he was even who her mother claimed.

Even after I married Walter, long after, the ladies of the parish, they thought they'd never let me forget who I was. Or where I'd come from. Small snubs, a curl of the lip, a turn of the eye. But in the long run it was I who had the ear of the Archbishop, wasn't it.

My career in the politics of church and home was something nobody could have predicted, when you thought of it. Especially when I got packed off to scrub the toilets and sweep the back stairs in the Glebe House when I was no more than fifteen years old. Taking orders from the beak-nosed housekeeper and told in no uncertain terms to keep out of the way of the priests. No matter what.

I didn't mind. I didn't know any better. And I certainly didn't want to run into any priests. I was scared of them then. But it was there in that Glebe

House that I saw books outside of the classroom for the first time. My job was to dust the tops of the things in the Library and to take each book from the shelves and dust behind it too. I remember sneezing a lot.

There I read Dante and St. Thomas Aquinas and *The Lives of the Saints*. All enough to convince me that the life I had, which didn't involve believing deeply in anything except getting to the end of the day, was still better than being beheaded or barbecued or crucified upside down or anything like that.

And then I discovered Cortés. And read again and again how six hundred Spaniards with guts and guile conquered the Aztec empire. The whole damn thing. And brought God to the Aztecs, Father Doyle pointed out when he saw me reading about it.

Brought them under control was what I figured. Brought under control hundreds of thousands of strong, well-organized people who didn't much like outsiders. And forced them to change the way they lived. And ended their empire. And claimed their land and riches. And swept away their religion. And more power to those Spaniards, if you ask me.

It wasn't without its light side, the whole thing, the conquest. Through-out the battles, the Spaniards and the Aztecs wore padded cotton armour. I remember thinking at the time, that was pretty funny. What could cotton armour ever protect you from? Depends, I guess, on what you're afraid of. In the case of arrows, I guess it worked pretty well. I thought a lot about that afterwards. Was it just because they believed in it?

Just reading about Cortés changed my way of thinking. I thought about the ladies of the parish and how they always figured they were a lot better than me, Helen Mooney from nowhere. Their fine clothes reminded me of cotton armour, protecting them from the revealing thoughts of others, if only they knew it. In time I got myself some cotton armour too. But not before I thought a lot about Cortés and his small band of soldiers in Mexico.

How many times did they nearly starve? How many of those soldiers were wounded? How often were they outnumbered? And they never gave up. But the thing that interested me most was how Cortés did it, since he and his soldiers were outnumbered, thousands to one, you know. Through guile, that's how. Always using guile, trickery and playing one group against the other. Just like me, in St. Anthony's Parish.

So you can see Cortés gave me a new perspective on life, knowing I could triumph, against all odds. Little Helen Nobody could become Some-body. I took a night course, and beat out every other student in the class. Me, Helen Mooney, who'd always lurked, tall and gangly, at the back of the classroom. I took another course. Bookkeeping. I still remember the teacher's approval of everything I did. She never could understand how the other night students could get so confused about what the assignment was or what was going to be on the exam, how they made foolish errors because they believed the wrong thing. I owe the technique of trickery to Cortés too.

Within two years, I was able to leave the Glebe House and get a job in the bank, beating out excellent competition that didn't understand about guile and the use of rumour. I learned to dress right. I bought my cotton armour at MacPherson's Ladies Wear. Fashionable. Concealing. Designed to protect the wearer and fool the opposition. It worked too. Two short years of strategy and privation and I married the manager of the bank. Walter Denniger. My Wally. My ambassador into the enemy camp.

But even though I had Wally, I always kept Cortés in my back pocket. Thirty years later he led me to my greatest victory and the sharp sweet three years where every decision was mine. Where the chance to humble and chastise came often but never without the aroma and taste of victory.

Where the troops followed me no matter what unless they wanted to face the consequences.

How often did I smilingly think of Cortés' reaction when I subtly rebuked a lady for insubordination, or raised my eyebrow, and asked for point of clarification during delicate negotiations or turned down the gangly adolescent children of the biggest troublemakers when they applied to use St. Anthony's hall for their dances.

If Cortés had been alive to see, surely he would have agreed the ladies of St. Anthony's were not unlike the conquered Aztecs, in more ways than one. Right down to the fancy feathers in their hats. Whenever I looked at those ladies in their fine clothes and feathers, I knew they could slip back into human sacrifice as soon as you turned your back.

They made fine enemies.

The memories of their eyes glittering with anger is all that keeps me going these days. Some of them made excellent opponents. Strong and proud. You could smell their cologne. Emeraude or Chanel, back then. Well worth conquering.

Better than that slithering Lila Winthrop, pale and pink, reeking of lily of the valley, always whispering behind her hand, breaking off in the middle of a word when you approached. Pretending to be so kind, so good, so generous, so unimpeachable . . . they said they had no choice but to elect her president in what would have been my fourth year.

No. That Lila Winthrop is more like, much more like, the cancer that invades my body, creeping, growing, pressing, always just out of reach of knife and painkiller. She always lurks in the back of my mind, nudging, probing, reminding.

Here comes Mindy with the bedpan. What a wheyfaced cow. What does my son see in her? The woman takes an eternity to do the slightest thing. Is that what hell would be like? Waiting an eternity for the bedpan? But it doesn't matter. What matters is what heaven will be like. I've earned my spot, let me tell you. The evidence of it is everywhere. Three, almost four, years as President of PLOW. Recognition from the pulpit, more times than you could even remember, for fundraising, organizing, making tough decisions, doing what needed to be done.

And more than just that. Dinners with the Archbishop. Receptions with tinkling crystal and fine wine. Didn't I shake hands with the Cardinal on more than one occasion? And think of my role during the Pope's visit. These things will count when the time comes.

"Took you long enough," I say.

"How are you?" she says.

"How do you think? I have a blue grapefruit eating my liver and I'm just terrific. Have you no feelings? The pain is unbearable."

I like it when her hands shake. That's the secret, just to get her on edge, just rattled enough but not so much she starts to cry and then next thing you know Peter's in the room talking about how much I'll like the palliative care at the Elizabeth Bruyère. Where they have the resources to look after me.

Resources indeed. He'd do it too. He's just like me. Does what he wants to. Does what he needs to. I'm proud of him.

But I am older and more cunning.

"I have your painkillers," Mindy says with only a small quiver.

I smile. Morphine.

"Don't worry," I say. "Things will get better. Soon you'll have my funeral to enjoy."

She gasps. It's lovely.

Her lips tremble. She bites the lower one.

Oh God, don't cry, you idiot woman. Have you no spine? I'd like to smack her, carrying on like that when Peter could step in at any moment.

Of course, she exaggerates her responses. There's some stubbornness deep down, otherwise she'd have given up the big bedroom with the bay window looking out over the birch and maple trees on the front lawn when I wanted it. But she didn't, even though Peter would have been willing. That's how I know she's not everything she pretends to be.

Good, she's got herself in control. Pain is beginning to get me down, sweeping out from the centre of the circle. Soaring to flame in my brain.

It's hard to breathe when the pills wear out. I don't really have the strength to battle with Peter.

Morphine.

The pills, the pills. Faster, faster . . . need them.

Water. Yes. Don't give in. Just the one, I remind myself. I force myself. Just the one and save the other under the tongue. Until she's gone.

She stays a long time. Lingering by the foot of the bed. Holding the full bedpan. It suits her, this line of work.

I want her out. Out so I can get the second pill from under my tongue and put it with the others. Before it melts. I don't know how much longer I'll be able to keep on saving the second pills. The pain never really leaves me now. I try to stand outside myself and observe my reactions to see what I can do to get control again. But the blast of pain sucks me back into myself. I lose myself to it.

I feel my sheets, warm and wet beneath me. Mindy will have to change them.

But I must do something.

"Call Doctor Graham. Tell him I need a much stronger dosage. The pain is unbearable. Get him on the phone now."

"But Mother . . ."

I want to scream don't call me mother you lazy stupid slut but even in my pain I know it's not a good move. Still I have to get rid of her.

"Or don't call him," I say, "don't call him to relieve my pain." I'm gasping for breath. Imagine knives finding soft places to twist in, it's like that. "The right dosage will only let me live longer, and we all know what a nuisance that would be."

I watch her through half-shut eyes. She always looks like she's been slapped, that one.

"I'll call him," she says.

"You do that."

She turns back when she reaches the door. "Oh, I almost forgot, I was able to reach the friend you asked me to phone. She said she'd love to come and visit you tomorrow. Remember? Lila Winthrop." She smiles when she closes the door behind her.

Of course, I remember. How could I forget? Didn't I ask her to call? Didn't I plan it? Didn't I arrange the whole thing? But oh my heart. My head. Lila Winthrop. Tomorrow! Just thinking about that pink and white vulture, flying in to gloat over my living corpse, I have no choice but to swallow the second pill. This time. This one time.

Lila Winthrop. It's only right for me to settle things with Lila. After all, did I not once have the ear of the Archbishop?

It takes eighteen minutes for the second pill to kick in. I know. I've timed it. I count the seconds. There is some satisfaction as I reach one thousand and eighty.

At last I can float on the cloud. Euphoria. Heaven will be like this. The floating. The sense of being well. The absence of pain. I am smiling when I lie there. The feelings last for hours, three, closer to four. Then the long stretching descent again, waiting for the flame knife to conquer my body.

This time it's worth the second pill.

I can finish my plans for Lila's visit.

The doctor is here. I see his face distorted, bending over. I hear his voice, talking to Mindy. Why ask her how I'm doing? What does she know? Scatterbrained would-be do-gooder. Why not ask me? I'll tell him, if he wants to know.

"The medication doesn't seem to be doing the job anymore," she says, twisting her hands.

Yes. That is the right message.

I'm feeling terrific, euphoric, flying through a sky of joy. But I don't want them to know that. Don't let the comfort, the pleasure, take you from your plan, Helen, I remind myself. Remember what you want.

I moan. And thrash.

They turn to look at me and turn away to talk.

Thank you. That tells me what they'd do if I really were moaning and squirming and trashing. If the hot knife were really doing its work.

For good measure, I let out a long, strangled, burbling scream. And try to sit up.

Through eyes more closed than open, I can still watch their reactions. The doctor moves toward the bed. I see Mindy holding back. One of her hands is over her mouth. The other one clutches her breast.

He sits on the edge of the bed.

"Can you hear me, Helen?"

"Of course, I can hear you," I blurt.

His eyes widen.

"In case you're forgetting, my liver's the problem, not my ears." It might be wise to temper my remarks but I feel the arrogant fool has it coming.

"Yes, of course. Mindy tells me the current dose of medication is not doing the job."

"Well, you can see that for yourself. The tumour must be bigger."

He nods. "The dose is already very high, Mrs. Denniger." I notice he's stopped calling me Helen.

"Really?" I say. "Are you afraid I'll become an addict?"

He jerks his head to look at me.

"Or maybe my long-term health will be at risk?"

He narrows his eyes.

I like to toy with them, these priests at the temple of medicine with their primitive totems and potions. I remember how Cortés turned the Aztec priests' beliefs against them, set them up for Christianity. Made off with their gold.

I meet his eyes. "What difference will it make," I say, "if one little old woman cuts out four hours of agony from her life every day? Who will be harmed by that?"

Out of the corner of my eye, I see Peter slip into the room. I hope he will have heard my argument. He likes that kind of thinking. I see him put his hand on Mindy's shoulder. She lays her head on his shoulder. At least she's pale and ugly looking from strain.

"You will have a hard time telling what is real, Mrs. Denniger, with a higher dose."

I bark out a laugh. "Reality is overrated, doctor. Take the word of someone with liver cancer."

I see him watching Peter and Mindy. They are watching him back.

"I think," he says, turning his fish-grey eyes to me, "you would be much better off in a palliative care unit."

You mean, she will be better off if I'm in a palliative care unit.

I say nothing. My heart thunders. I haven't the strength to conquer new territory. I want to stay here with my war trophies. In my own home.

"They have special training. They have the right staff and facilities. You will be much more comfortable there."

"Really," I say. "Staff? Facilities? Is it the same as your family? Can they duplicate the feeling of being in your own home? The memories, the air, the feelings?"

I see Mindy wilt a bit. Why won't I just slink off and die in peace, she's probably thinking, so she can air out the house and burn the mattress and be in charge again.

The doctor compresses his lips. And what is he thinking? That I should have some consideration and die quickly and without fuss surrounded by paid strangers?

Peter's face firms up. I can see his decision written there. I can feel it.

"This is my mother's home," he says.

I see Mindy turn from him and struggle to pull herself together. Smothering the hot tears. Trying to look like it's my best interests she has in mind.

I manage a brave smile through the pain I am not feeling. I reach out and squeeze Peter's hand.

"My home," I whisper and close my eyes.

My plan, I think, will work out fine.

Cotton armour, that's the secret. I have mine. A silky white cotton nightie with handmade lace on the square collar and cuffs. Spotless. Mindy has gone out and purchased new white sheets. With eyelet ruffles and matching pillow cases and coverlet. All with white eyelet ruffles.

Of course, she'd hesitated. Probably thinking what good is it to spend money on the old lady when she can't have more than a month to hang on to life if she's lucky.

"You might as well spend some of my money on me when I'm alive," I said to her. "You'll get enough when I'm dead."

Two spots of red coloured her cheeks as she left the room to go shopping. She did not shut the door softly.

I'm sure she was thinking about how much work it would be to get stains from the sheets, but that was not my problem.

Mindy brings the phone to my bed, as requested. When she leaves the room, I order flowers from the florist. A showy bouquet of peach roses, mums, and baby's breath. I have them put on Peter's Visa. Why not? Sixty dollars less for Mindy after I'm gone. They ask if I want a message on the card. Oh yes, I say, and give the bishop's name.

I call Peter and Mindy's travel agent. I use the Visa number again to book a tour of the south of France. Two weeks away. Yes, I understand it will be more expensive at such short notice.

I send Mindy out for sachets. And those air fresheners you plug into the wall socket. The scent of roses, I tell her.

It has worked out well. I've had a sponge bath. And scented talc. I have managed to have my hair done. It almost killed me and it cost nearly forty dollars to have that girl come to the house and do my hair in the bedroom, but it was worth it.

Mindy has even ironed my cotton underwear as I requested. She got a look on her face like the trout my husband used to haul from the lake. Didn't want to iron someone else's underwear, I guess. Her problem, not mine. I have the cool, soft, smooth cotton I need next to me. Protection from the treachery and cunning of my rival.

I check the mirror. You can hardly see my illness on my face.

Mindy has set up the silver tea service and china cups. Just within my reach. She goes to sink into the flowered guest chair.

I do not want her hanging around the room while I prepare myself to meet my old enemy.

"Are those the best cookies you could find?" I say. "Don't we have any decent shortbread?"

She scurries from the room and down the hall. Swish, swish. I am alone.

I make myself ready to face Lila Winthrop.

She sits there. Fresh and crisp in her golf clothes. Smiling the snake smile I remember so well. The smile of the good little girl who has gotten everything worked out to her satisfaction, with the help of her orthodontist and her accountant. I can almost read her thoughts. She is thinking I might have conquered her in my parish initiatives, turned her into an unwilling captive, robbed her of glory, especially with the Annual Summer Fête and the Fall Tea and Sale, and the Christmas Parish Pageant. Cut off her ways of complaining, turned her allies against her with the right information, the right tones, the right raised eyebrow. Clipped her wings. Until.

Until she triumphed by guile and won the Presidency of PLOW. The worst day of my life. I hated her. I hate her now. I work back in my mind and calculate most likely that's the day it started, the cancer, a small speck, a single cell turned white hot by hate, glowing. Growing.

And look at her. She is certainly thinking she will triumph again in the end because, after all, I am dying of hate and she is off to play nine holes, crisp in her cotton. Pink cotton. A soft deceptive pink, like cotton candy. Very tricky.

But I have cotton too. Cotton armour.

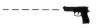

Mindy is back with the shortbread, hovering, even after Lila is seated in the upholstered visitor's chair with the peony design in burgundy and white. Mindy hovers, practically twitching. I can't stand that. She makes me edgy when she hovers. She has already set out the silver service on the campaign table near my bed.

"We don't need anything else," I tell her. "Come back later. You can serve us some fresh tea in about twenty minutes."

Mindy opens her mouth and closes it again. Really, she looks more like a muskie than a trout.

I can hear her polyester swishing as she moves along the hallway. Silly thing. She's never been smart enough for cotton. Wouldn't recognize what it could do for her anyway.

Not like Lila. Lila turns her head when I am speaking to Mindy. It's her little way of letting me know she's much too well bred to listen to orders being given to the help. Fine with me. Out of the corner of my eye, I see her admiring the flowers.

"Aren't they lovely?" I say. "And so fragrant."

Of course she has to lean over and sniff the fragrance. But with the air of humouring me. She must have practised that look for years. She's much better at it than she used to be. Closer, I think, get closer. Yes.

She has spotted the bishop's name on the card. Her head snaps back. Bingo.

She doesn't see my hand flash over the pink china cup, just high enough, but never touching it.

"Very nice," she says. She doesn't give me the satisfaction of mentioning the bishop's name. Or letting on she's noticed. That's fine. I wouldn't respect her if she did.

And hell would freeze over before I would be so unclassy as to mention it.

"Mindy has left us this very nice tea," I say.

"Yes, indeed." I notice she's looking a little pinched around the mouth.

The cups are Royal Albert. My two favourite from Wally's mother's collection. The pink one has white lacy edges and the blue ones has tiny flowers.

"Which cup would you prefer?" I ask. I make sure she sees me eye the pink one myself. I reach to pass her the blue one just in case she doesn't catch on. She sees all right. She sees my hand shaking too. I actually have to make it shake. I've never felt surer of anything before. Strength floods me.

But I don't let on. Instead, I lean back on the pillow and gasp, as if the effort of reaching for the blue cup has just about done me in.

"I do love pink," she says, as if I didn't know that. "Matches my outfit too."

"It suits you."

She flicks her eyes to my trembling hand.

"May I pour?"

I hesitate. "Of course," I say, pretending to mask my tiny disappointment.

She makes sure I see her strong, steady hands, grip the handle and the lid of the silver pot, pouring with grace and just a little more flourish than the situation actually calls for. She passes me my blue cup with a smile, synthetic pity in her eyes.

As her fingers close around the handle of her pink cup, and she raises it to her lips, I pick up my blue cup and sip. It is all I can do, to keep from howling.

She's lying there, that pink skirt pulled up when she fell. Her mouth is open. Her eyes bulge. You can see her legs, gnarled a bit with lumpy blue veins. Not very pretty.

I smile at that. But internally where such smiles belong.

The only irritation is the sound of Mindy bawling. No sense of proper behaviour, that one, never did have.

Peter is conferring with the doctor. They've both let their customary "I'm in charge here" looks slip a bit. This is bad, this is troublesome and time-consuming, they are thinking. Lila Winthrop's inconsiderate demise will mean a lot of forms to be filled in. A real nuisance.

I slip back into the sheets. I sigh.

Peter and the doctor turn to face me.

I've paid enough taxes in my life, so it's good to see them getting put to work. Fairly quickly, the police figure it out. The dregs of Lila's tea, still pooled in the cup, contain a startling amount of morphine. Enough to knock off the entire block, probably. Paid for in a sea of pain. Dozens of pills held back under my tongue. Dozens of hot knives twisted in my body, to make those pills available, but worth it. Well worth it.

The police have the cup. They will have found only Mindy's and Lila's prints on it. My cup. My favourite china cup. Peter will know that and perhaps mention it to the investigating officer. But never mind, just in case, I have let it slip into the conversation. "But it was my cup, officer, she liked the look of it. Naturally, I let her use it. She was my guest, after all."

Even the doctor with his fish-grey eyes, I know he would rather it be me. Better if I were dead, since I'm a quite a bother now. I can tell he hates to see me when we both know he's helpless against this disease. And, of course, he much prefers Mindy to me. But even he has to admit, I never asked for extra medication. Mindy was the one who asked for the dose.

Mindy, the long-suffering daughter-in-law, waiting on the nasty old lady hand and foot. Why not liberate herself from such drudgery and take a nice little trip or two with the inheritance? I mention to the police officer that Mindy had often talked of going to the south of France. Of course, she will deny it. Because it never happened.

I have many nurses now. Round the clock. Much better if you ask me. They do what they're told. I just have to remember how far I can go.

For days now, I have heard the sound of Mindy's wailing and snuffling. It brings great satisfaction. Who knows what more entertainment will come from all this?

But my day nurse is here, plump and pretty. She gives a lovely sponge bath. And I'm set up in the big front bedroom now, with the bay window looking over the silver birches and red maples on the front lawn. I can't be expected to stay in the room where such a terrible thing happened to my friend. Peter won't hear of it.

Even the pain is under control, since I don't have to hide one out of every two pills. Everything is much improved.

The nurse sits herself down. She reaches over to hold my hand. She's the type to be a faithful retainer, this one.

"They're taking her in," she says, squeezing my hand, gently, gently.

"Not really?" I say.

She nods, oozing compassion. She must have had a course in it.

"They're sure . . . she did it?"

"I don't know. But they must be. They're here for her."

I shake my head, as if I'm almost too weak to move. "It was supposed to be me. It was in my favourite cup. She had no reason to want to harm poor Lila."

The nurse squeezes my hand.

No smile mars my face. Cortés would be proud of me.

I pull my eyelet-fringed cotton armour up around me and close my eyes.

I sleep in victory.

Mystery Men

Here's to the men

and the mysteries they write.

We all still enjoy them—

especially at night.

Joy Hewitt Mann

Most of the authors are members of Sisters in Crime, Capital Crime Writers, and Mystery Writers of America.

Elizabeth Syme has been writing full-time since her retirement six years ago. Her first novel, Kiss Me Goodnight, a contemporary romance, was published by Zebra Books, New York, in November, 1993. Earlier in her career, Elizabeth had a mystery television play, Drop Dead, produced on BBC-TV. She has two short stories scheduled for publication in 1995.

Joan Boswell divides her time between writing, painting, and running an Art Gallery in Ottawa. As an artist, she exhibits her work in Ottawa and Toronto. She writes mystery short stories, and mystery novels for adults and children.

Victoria Cameron was a freelance writer for the Smiths Falls EMC, Canadian Holstein, and Ontario Milk Producer for ten years. She is the author of two non-fiction books, From Heel to Finish: The System of Ghent for the Nineties, and Don't Tell Anyone, But . . . UFO Experiences in Canada. She also writes Young Adult mystery novels.

Rose DeShaw is a columnist with the Mystery Review, former member of PWAC, and was for twenty years a columnist with the Anglican Journal. Her writing has appeared in national newspapers and magazines in Canada and the U.S.. She is currently published in the anthology Eating Apples; Knowing Women's Lives. She owns a book store in Kingston.

Melanie Fogel has an abiding interest in the forensic aspects of criminal investigation. She is a partner in THETICS, a company specializing in writing and editorial services, and is a founding editor of STORYteller Magazine. She won third prize in the 1994 Ottawa Citizen "Write Now!" mystery short story competition.

Barbara Fradkin was born in Montreal and now lives in Ottawa. She works as a child psychologist for a local school board. She's been writing stories since she was six. Now, she writes mystery short stories and adult detective novels.

Audrey Jessup is a native of England who emigrated to Canada in 1948. She is a founding member of Ottawa Romance Writers and Capital Crime Writers. In 1994, she won second prize in the Ottawa Citizen "Write Now!" mystery short story competition. Currently, she is working on a mystery novel. She volunteers with Friends of the National Gallery, and QUAIL (Quebec Association for Independent Living).

Mary Jane Maffini won the 1994 Ottawa Citizen "Write Now!" mystery short story competition for her first Grim Reaper tale, "Death Before Donuts." Her short story "Naked Truths" appeared in Cold Blood V. She is Director of Information Services at Canada Institute for Scientific and Technical Information at the National Research Council. She is a member of the Canadian Library Association.

Joy Hewitt Mann has published over 150 poems in both literary quarterlies and national magazines, including Amelia, Blindstone, and Mature Living in the U.S., and Carleton Arts Review, Whetstone, and Women's Education Des Femmes in Canada. In 1992 and 1993, she was the recipient of the Gala Award for Poetry, sponsored by the Midwest Poetry Review. She is editor of a literary anthology and a writers' newsletter, and runs a collectables store. Her mystery stories appear in Hardboiled magazine.

Marguerite McDonald has been a nun and a network television reporter. Her assignments for CBC radio and television have taken her to every province in Canada and to Ethiopia, Central America, and the Middle East. She is an avid sea-kayaker and outdoorsperson. Currently, she gives the news on CBC Radio every morning.

Sue Pike is an Ottawa freelance writer and editor who plots mysteries in her spare time. She has prepared booklets for the United Way and scripts for TVOntario. Her short story "Still Waters" appeared in Cold Blood V.

Linda Wiken is a journalist and works for the Ottawa Board of Education in community outreach. As a volunteer with the Ottawa Police, she writes a weekly crime statistics column for local newspapers, and edits a bimonthly newsletter, Cop Talk.

For more copies of

The *Ladies Killing Circle*

send $17.95 plus $3.00 to cover
GST, shipping and handling to:

GENERAL STORE PUBLISHING HOUSE
1 Main Street, Burnstown, Ontario
K0J 1G0

Telephone 1-800-465-6072
Fax 613-432-7184